The Ascent of
Eli Israel

The Ascent of
Eli Israel

And Other Stories

JON PAPERNICK

Arcade Publishing • New York

FIRST EDITION

This is a work of fiction. Names, places, characters, and incidents are either products of the author's imagination or are used fictitiously.

"Lucky Eighteen" contains excerpts from the poems "A Majestic Love Song" and "Love Song" by Yehuda Amichai, translated by Yehuda Amichai and Ted Hughes. Used by permission of the estate of Yehuda Amichai.

Excerpt from *The Hogg Poems* by Barry Callaghan used by permission of the author.

"For as Long as the Lamp Is Burning" first appeared in the *Sarah Lawrence Review;* "An Unwelcome Guest" first appeared in *The Reading Room*; "Malchyk" first appeared in *Exile.*

ISBN 1-55970-619-8
Library of Congress Control Number 2002105002
Library of Congress Cataloging-in-Publication information is available.

Published in the United States by Arcade Publishing, Inc., New York
Distributed by AOL Time Warner Book Group

Visit our Web site at www.arcadepub.com

10 9 8 7 6 5 4 3 2 1

Designed by API

EB

PRINTED IN THE UNITED STATES OF AMERICA

Contents

For my mother. For my father.

so you go you see
to a city
suspended somewhere
between prayer
and the hanging rope

where most men
have
the faith
but few
have hope

Barry Callaghan,
The Hogg Poems

Malchyk

On the Fifth Day of Iyar, in the Jewish Year of 5709 (May 4th, 1949, by our calendar), which was the first anniversary of Israel's Declaration of Independence and attainment of statehood, a rabbi in Jerusalem suggested that women who bore children . . . should name their infants Teshua (Redemption) if they were girls, and Herut (Freedom) if they were boys. . . . Later on the semantics of maturity may cast a shadow across the word(s), but on the Fifth Day of Iyar, 5709, it meant only one thing to every man, woman and child in Israel, and they thronged the roads, filled the cities, shot fireworks into the air, paraded, applauded, cheered and sang in freedom's honor.

Irwin Shaw, *Report on Israel*

Pirkl slept an uneasy sleep and dreamed again of his father's death.

A dark legionnaire appeared at the head of his mattress, whispering in his ear between machine-gun fire and the incessant boom of the big guns sounding off throughout the city. "The Grand Mufti himself sent me." Flares and tracers from the sky flashed across the stranger's beard, his black eyes burned electric green. "The quarter has been sacked," the Arab said.

Pirkl closed his eyes tight, *go a-way, go a-way, don't come back 'til Judgment Day.*

"Beautiful boy," the stranger said, stroking Pirkl's cheek with an empty shell casing. There was blood on the legionnaire's chest, and Pirkl touched a deep stain on his uniform shaped like the Shield of David. "His brave blood," the stranger answered and a tear rolled from his cheek. Pirkl drank the tears down as they poured from the stranger's face and the Ras el 'Ain pipeline was flowing again with cool springwater.

He awoke to his mother stroking his hair. "Shhh," she said, mopping sweat from his brow. Only a small kerosene lamp burned against the early morning darkness. Her eyes were ringed in black. She was as gaunt as a baby bird and wore a blue bandanna around her neck. A soldier with a bandaged head groaned from a stretcher not five feet away. "Shhh," she repeated, holding a small tin cup to Pirkl's lips. "Drink."

He sat up in bed as a whistling shell fired from the Katamon neighborhood crashed in a nearby street. "I'm going to find Abba," Pirkl said.

When the Jewish state was declared two weeks earlier, Pirkl had followed his mother to the sixth floor of their apartment house, where an Arab Legion shell had crashed through the roof of a neighbor's flat. The shell did not explode but had smashed a large jagged hole in the ceiling. White moonlight poured in through the opening, lighting the room with a silvery glow. Pirkl watched his mother step through the shattered glass and plaster and thought she looked like an angel. The air was thick and hot and smelled of crushed stone as Pirkl kicked up the white dust into clouds, imagining heaven.

Someone's wireless set crackled loudly from a lower floor and echoed through the darkened stairwell and the now-abandoned apartment. "This is *Kol Hamagen HaIvri,* the broadcasting service of the Haganah, calling on a wavelength of thirty-five to thirty-eight meters or seven to seven-point-five megacycles. Here is our English transmission. . . ." His mother pulled a bookshelf up to the hole and climbed the shelves, disappearing a moment later through the twisted steel into the hot night air. "Come, Malchyk," she called. Pirkl bristled at the childish nickname that had been his since he was six years old, and began to climb, careful not to step on the leather-bound commentaries. The broadcaster read from David Ben-Gurion's Declaration of Independence, his voice catching on the words, ". . . by virtue of the natural and historic right of the Jewish people and on the strength of the resolution of the General Assembly of the United Nations, hereby declares the establishment of the Jewish state in Palestine, to be called Israel. . . ." Pirkl repeated the word "Israel" as he pulled himself out onto the rooftop.

His mother took his hand, and he wanted to pull away and say, *I don't need to hold your hand anymore,* but realized for the first time as she squeezed him tightly that *she* needed his hand. The bombing that had gone on nightly for weeks continued; incandescent blood streaks across the sky, the east flickering like an undecided sunrise, gray plumes of smoke climbing into the night. "Do you think we will have a king at last?"

"I don't know," she said wearily.

"Father is there?" Pirkl asked, pointing to the smoke seething from within the besieged Old City. Only the Arab Legion's artillery answered.

He had not seen his father since the *hamsiin* began, when the hot sirocco wind blew from the desert at the start of May draining the life and color out of everything.

"How can they fight during the *hamsiin*?" Pirkl had asked his mother.

"Yihye tov," his mother answered, "It will be all right."

Pirkl knew his father was there within the twisting rabbit warren streets defending the ancient Jewish Quarter. He had heard rumors of a Haganah unit disguised as an Arab Legion marching band who arrived at Damascus Gate blasting their trumpets. When the gates opened Pirkl imagined his father's kaffiyeh dropping to the ground, his trumpet magically transformed into a Sten gun, his voice raised singing, "Rifle on rifle our guns will salute / Bullet on bullet our guns will shoot." His father had taught Pirkl the "Song of the Barricades," how to hurl stones at the British, and how to fashion a grenade out of an empty jam tin with bits of broken glass, shrapnel, matches, and gunpowder. It seemed like years since Pirkl had helped his father to sandbag windows on Gaza Road.

"Father is there," Pirkl said, "I know he is there."

A half-dozen smoke rockets blasted up into the sky from the Old City just two kilometers away. His mother turned her back on the distress signals and did not answer.

The wireless continued to echo throughout the dark stairwell, "All laws enacted under the Palestine White Paper of the British government, and all laws deriving from it are declared null and void. . . ." Pirkl felt his way down the stairs, following his mother's breathing. And then someone was jamming the wireless transmission and a voice cut in laughing, "We will drink blood from your skulls. Into the sea, Jews!"

That night Pirkl began to dream about his father's death.

Pirkl slipped into his dirty overalls, which hadn't been cleaned since water-rationing began. He placed his knitted cap onto his head and tied his shoes. The morning sun was coming up blue through the slats of the iron shutters. His mother took the tin cup from his side and tried to smile, touching his cheek. The soldier with the bandaged head sighed deeply in his sleep. Tsrili had been injured defending Ramat Rahel and was anxious to return to the battle but fell down dizzy and confused every time he stood up. Pirkl enjoyed singing Palmach marching songs with the injured soldier but was tired of hanging around the iodine-smelling apartment plugging wounds and beating away buzzing clouds of flies.

Just the night before Pirkl had stood showing off with his girlfriend Hannah, wearing an oversized helmet on his head in the middle of the living room. He declared in his most official-sounding baritone, "Pirkl of Rehavia you are conscripted in the name of Zion."

"What are your duties, brave one?" Hannah said, batting her eyelashes dramatically.

"To save Jerusalem!" Tsrili shouted from his stretcher before losing consciousness.

Now his grandmother entered with a crust of bread in one hand, a satchel thrown over her right shoulder. She handed him the bread, which was thinly covered with bitter chocolate spread. Pirkl gobbled it down.

"Good morning," she said.

"The reinforcements are ready," he answered.

"You make a handsome soldier."

His mother interrupted, "Pirkl is not a soldier. He's too young."

"I'm older than David when he killed Goliath."

"Don't talk nonsense."

"What is he, a worthless *shmatte,* a worthless old rag?" his grandmother said. "Let him go. Every man must fight for Jerusalem. He will soon be bar mitzvah. He smells like a man," she said, pinching her sharp nose.

"You belong at home . . ." his mother began.

"But what about the brave Trumpeldor?" Pirkl shot back.

"He was killed at Tel Hai," his mother answered, shaking her head.

"Defending Tel Hai," his grandmother said. "He didn't die in vain."

"You're not going to look for your father. Promise me," his mother said.

Pirkl smiled, but didn't say anything. He thought of the Russian-born, one-armed Joseph Trumpeldor. His father's hero.

Pirkl's grandmother winked at him.

"All right," his mother said. "Come straight back, Malchyk! Just go to the barricade. Hold this above your head," she said, handing him a piece of white muslin cloth. "Hold it high so the snipers can see. Look for the Red Cross, leave the package, tell them it is for those trapped in the city. They will listen to a child."

"Let him go!" his grandmother said. Though he was just five feet tall, she still had to reach up to kiss his cheek. "Be strong and brave," she said.

His grandmother had packed a small satchel filled to the top with two loaves of stale bread, three cans of asparagus soup, a tin of chocolate spread, a package of dried fruit, some potatoes, a cup of dried beans, sweet halvah, candles, a blanket, week-old copies of *Ha'aretz* and some small dark jars which contained a liquid that must have been medicine.

His heart quickened, he could feel it boiling in his chest as he bounced down the stairs. The full weight of the *hamsiin* hit him as he stepped out into the magic pink light of morning. He walked around behind the apartment house and emptied the bag onto the ground next to a jagged bowl-shaped crater where a twenty-five-pounder had hit one night during heavy shelling, and dug in the dry earth where Tsrili, the soldier injured at Ramat Rahel, would later be buried.

When his mother was busy tending to the wounded, he had hidden a pair of three-inch Davidka mortar shells made out of old pipes, a few dozen Enfield rifle bullets, three bayonets, and the pièce de résistance, a round Thompson submachine gun magazine. He held the magazine to his chest, like a stack of precious 78 rpm records that his mother used to play on the phonograph. And for a moment, he saw his parents dancing and laughing in their living room, his mother's head thrown back with such joy, he could hardly recognize her now.

He pressed the bullets into the stale bread until they all disappeared into the now-heavy loaves; wrapped the bayonets thickly in the old newspapers, and swaddled the Thompson magazine in the blanket, piling dried fruit on top in case he was stopped and asked the contents of his bag. Pirkl imagined his two rockets, marked "Dear King Abdullah" and "For Haj Amin Mufti," hitting their targets squarely on top of their heads. Two shells can win the war, he thought, and pictured himself riding along King George V Avenue in an open car with Hannah at his side. His reverie was interrupted by the thump of shelling from the east.

Hannah lived in the next apartment house with her mother and stepfather who were Communists. She was the first girl his own age Pirkl had ever thought was pretty, with her long almond-shaped face, spinning green eyes, and brand-new breasts. He liked her for that, but he also liked the fact that her parents let her do as she wished. Sometimes in the evenings, during the bombing, she would throw rocks at Pirkl's window and he would meet her in the stairwell where they would kiss in the thick darkness. She promised soon that Pirkl could touch her *there*.

He gathered up the cans of soup, the potatoes and the beans, the chocolate spread, some dried fruit, and even the sweet halvah, and left them on the doorstep outside her flat. She had gotten so skinny, Pirkl thought, so light, he could have carried her on his back all the way to the Old City. He heard her stepfather behind the door glumly singing the "Internationale." Pirkl ran off to gather his satchel humming "Hatikvah," The Hope, the nation's anthem.

Skipping over shell craters and tangled telephone wires, counting broken windows and garbage piles, Pirkl continued humming as he went. He counted in Hebrew, and then English, then in Russian. Sometimes he mixed the three together.

Farther on down the road Pirkl could see the barricade, and behind that no-man's-land. A high nasal voice called to him from behind a low stone wall, "Hey, boy. Curlyhead! Come here." Pirkl stopped beneath an almond tree and adjusted the heavy bag on his back, about to move on.

"Boy, you are going to the Ancient City?"

"Who wants to know?" Pirkl asked.

"I know," the voice said. "I know."

And then, the oldest man Pirkl had ever seen stood up from behind the wall. He was barefoot and dressed entirely in black, with a black felt hat tilted back on his giant head. He had a wild white beard, wispy like dry grass, and his eyes were pale and glassy.

"Come here, boy," the holy man said, holding out his long bony hand.

Pirkl could see the veins in his hand so clearly they might have been above the skin. His back was hunched and he smelled of old books and damp soil. And then he spoke and his breath smelled of fish bones that had been almost picked clean.

"You are going to the Ancient City."

Pirkl put his bag down. "Do you live there?"

"Yes."

"But you ran?" Pirkl said.

The holy man laughed, but instead of a laugh it was a breath and not a breath, as if he had one of those fish bones caught in his throat. "I ran?"

"How long did you live there?"

"Five hundred years," the man answered, then wheezed and laughed again. "Your name, boy."

Pirkl told him. He could not stop looking into the man's glassy cataracted eyes, dreamy like cracked crystal balls.

"Your mother?"

He could hear heavy machine-gunning in the distance and the savage boom, boom, boom of the bigger guns.

"Rosa," Pirkl said.

"Take this," the holy man said, slipping a small silver amulet into Pirkl's hand. He gripped his arm tight and did not let go. Pirkl closed his eyes and began to sway. He thought he felt the old man reach into his overall pockets, but he ignored it, thinking the poor man was simply searching for hidden food. The old man's pink tongue rolled around in his tooth-less mouth trying to form words, his voice high-pitched and broken: "In the name of Shaddai who created heaven and earth and in the name of the angel . . ." He was shaking faster and Pirkl felt an ache in his groin and a vibration down his spine. "In the name of Pirkl son of Rosa, protect him in all of his two-hundred and forty-eight organs against danger and the two-edged sword. Help him, deliver him, save him . . ."

He felt the man's soft hand sliding against him and electricity buzzing down all the knuckles of his spine and out into his rib cage. "Vanquish and bring low those who rise against him. May all who seek his harm be destroyed, humbled, smashed so that not a limb remains whole . . ." He felt a fire in his legs and arms now, burning through his veins and arteries, a white fire cleansing his very soul. "Save him, deliver him from all sorcery, from wicked men, from sudden death. Grant him grace, and love and mercy before the throne of God and before all beings who behold him." The old man let go of Pirkl's arm, and his eyes snapped open. He continued to chant, his stinking pink mouth an open wound, "Yah Yah Yah Yau Yau Yau Yah Zebaot. Amen Amen Amen." And all at once the electricity was gone and Pirkl felt his body shiver as if he had exploded. The man again broke into a sepulchral laugh and Pirkl noticed the man had wet his pants. He felt damp in his own pants. He had been tricked by a madman.

"Pirkl, Pirkl, beautiful boy," the man cackled, taking the amulet back into his long bony hands. "Pirkl, Pirkl."

He walked away laughing, and Pirkl grabbed him by the shoulder not concerned anymore that the old man might crumble into dust.

"Why did you touch me?"

"For luck," the old man said. "For luck."

"I don't need luck," Pirkl said, sickened and angry.

"You want to die as a lamb?"

"I'm not going to die."

"Child, you exaggerate your own importance. Death is in the air." And with that, he raised his nose to the sky, sniffing, his nose hairs waving like tiny spider's legs.

"Come with me," he said, sliding a finger into his tooth-less mouth.

Then Pirkl said a word so foul that he had never said it aloud before. The old man's face dropped and he began to shuffle away.

"If you must go," he said, color rising to his pallid face, "enter through the small door, my little dung beetle."

When Pirkl reached the barricade, he removed the bayonets from his heavy satchel, throwing them on the ground in disgust. He was sticky and felt something dripping down his leg and wiped it up with the gauze his mother had given him to ward off sniper fire. Through a peephole, he could see a park where he once played, strewn with barbed wire and rough cement blocks. He didn't smell death in the air, only burned gunpowder and dust. His father, the best person in the whole world, was only a few hundred meters away, inside that stony prison. Pirkl felt tears surge up from his belly and he wanted to run to him as fast as his legs could carry him.

Though it was still early morning, a white sun made the whole world look like an overexposed photograph. Pirkl removed his wool cap, and standing on top of his own small shadow, peered through the peephole again. The Old City. "I can dribble a football that far," he thought. "Kick it right through Jaffa Gate."

Pirkl made a bet with himself as he walked along the barricade that he would not be spotted moving across no-man's-land. He was simply too small to be of any consideration, too much a part of the landscape to be noticed. With the satchel humped up on his back, covered with dust, he might be mistaken for a camel.

He found a breach in the barrier and slipped through,

scraping his arm on a bracelet of barbed wire, and began walking toward the flames and pounding shells. "This is easy," he thought, heading toward the well-fortified Jaffa Gate. He had just begun whistling "Song of the Barricades" when he heard a bullet ricochet past him, then another. Pirkl could not see where the marksman was shooting from, but dove face-first onto the ground and crawled behind a pile of stones, closing his eyes. His heart beat hard behind his eyelids.

With his face pressed into the dry earth, Pirkl thought of Hannah. He once told her he would die if he didn't touch her *there*. And now he was sure he would die.

"You won't die," she had said, her lips against his, her words disappearing into his mouth.

He spoke back into her mouth, "I will!"

"No you won't. If I let you touch it now, what is there to look forward to?"

"Lots of things," Pirkl said, kissing her dry lips.

"No," she said. "You will *have* to live. So you can touch it later."

"Please."

"Not now," she said, placing his hands on her behind and pulling him closer. She smelled of kerosene and sweat.

Pirkl wanted to tell Hannah that he loved her, he loved her so much, but said, "When do you think my father will come home?"

"I don't know," she said. "Stalin took my father when I was three. His father died in a pogrom in Dokszyce. But don't worry," she said. "You can get a new father."

. . .

What would happen if he died in no-man's-land? Would Hannah cry for him and call him brave and wish she had let him touch her, Pirkl wondered. Sweat poured down his neck, tickling him, the way Hannah's fingers did. His mouth was full of soot, he didn't dare raise his head. Would his mother know the moment a bullet ripped through his body? Would she feel his last breath fade away the way she felt his first breath when he came into the world?

Some dried apricots spilled out of the satchel onto the ground. "My last meal on earth, and I don't even like apricots." Then a horrifying thought crept into Pirkl's mind: If my father is dead, would I know? He is defending the Old City and bombs are falling. Can he walk between a million raindrops and not get wet?

The sniper must have thought he had hit his target, for the ricocheting bullets stopped, as did the bombing within the Old City. Only the odd report of machine-gun fire echoed from within the walls. Pirkl removed the awkward Thompson magazine from his bag and laid it beside the pile of rocks, pushed himself up off the ground and ran as fast as he could back toward the barricade and the breach he had slipped through. Not a shot was fired.

Down by the Yemin Moshe neighborhood he decided to try again. *Of course* Jaffa Gate, the main gate in the west, would be heavily guarded. It was stupid to try, Pirkl thought. And Zion Gate, too, was a fortress. But the little gate! He peered up at the city and he could see fires burning from within the Jewish Quarter. The bombing had stopped.

In the winter his father had taken him to Montefiore's Windmill at the top of Yemin Moshe, which offered a majestic view of the Old City and the valley below. To the south, his father pointed out the British High Commissioner's "Government House" on a gray hilltop. He chuckled at the irony that the seat of the mandatory government would be located on the Hill of Evil Counsel. They looked out on the walled city that seemed to be almost buried in the mountains, and down below, the Hinnom Valley, or Gehenna. His father told him that in ancient times, pagans had built a shrine to Moloch, an angry god hungry for human flesh. Children were sacrificed in that valley, and their blood flowed all the way to the Dead Sea. Pirkl asked his father if children were still sacrificed. He said, no, not if they were good.

Now he was in that valley, making his way across the burnished earth to the Old City, and the Union Jack was gone from that gray hill, replaced by mortars and cannons. He imagined walking over the bones of children burned in the bronze arms of Moloch. Down he went and he heard goats bleating in the distance and he heard the mournful clanging of their bells. Across the valley he counted ten white dots moving slowly among the twisted olive trees. Every once in a while he heard the rat-tat of gunfire from within the city.

He wanted to eat some of the dried fruit as he walked along, but was afraid he would not have enough when he reached his father. His bag was lighter now, and he cursed himself for leaving behind the Thompson magazine. He only had the two mortars for King Abdullah and the Grand Mufti, as well as the two loaves of bullet-loaded bread. Loose dried fruit tumbled around in his satchel. He could make out tiny figures on the ramparts as he passed Mount Zion and the mighty edifice of Dormition Abbey. "Moloch, come out wherever you are," Pirkl thought defiantly. "I'm walking through your valley."

Pirkl climbed the steep eastern slope of the valley on his way to the little gate of which the madman had spoken. Pirkl smiled. Dung Gate, the smallest and most insignificant entrance into the city, so small that a man on horseback would have to dismount to enter, a gate that once served as an open sewer in times of antiquity. Dung Gate, the closest gate to the Jewish Quarter and his father.

He stepped through the barbed wire and dust and rubble, sweating furiously. He was so thirsty his head began to buzz. Still not a sound from within the city, but the smell of smoke and death burned in his nose. He removed the thin blanket from within his satchel and wrapped it around his face like a kaffiyeh.

A solitary legionnaire sitting languidly in an opening above the gate waved and said, *"Marhaba."* Pirkl smiled and said the same.

The gate was even smaller than Pirkl remembered. He noticed the decorous Star of David carved above it and mumbled the Sheheheyanu, a prayer said on joyous occasions that he remembered hearing old men muttering.

Skirting the Arab Muhgrabi Quarter, he walked uphill toward the battered cupola of the Tiferet Israel Synagogue. The narrow streets were littered with rotting vegetables, twisted bed frames, scattered clothing, smashed crockery, books, photographs, broken furniture, rubble, and all the debris one might have acquired in a lifetime. A terrible sadness rose up from within Pirkl; he wanted to scream out and curse and stamp his feet

THE ASCENT OF ELI ISRAEL

He came to a small storefront where a young Arab sat at a round table.

"Hello," the Arab said in English.

Pirkl ignored him and continued to walk.

"'Hello,' I said. Come back or I will shout that there is a Jew still alive."

Pirkl froze.

"The Jews are surrendering today," the Arab said to him.

Pirkl shook his head and thought of his handsome father and him singing: "On the barricades we will meet at last / And lift freedom on high from the chains of the past."

"You're lying," Pirkl said.

"You have lost the Holy City."

"No," Pirkl said.

"An Arab flag flies over the Haram."

"It can't be," Pirkl said, and then thought, "We have taken Katamon and Bakaa and Talbiyeh. We've recaptured Ramat Rahel."

"You look thirsty. I have water and some dates."

Pirkl sat down, suddenly exhausted, deflated, and thirsty.

"This morning, two rabbis carried a white bedsheet between two broomsticks. They have surrendered."

"We would never give up Jerusalem," Pirkl said, trailing off, ". . . rather die."

"What is in the bag?'

Pirkl hesitated. "Some dried fruit."

"Good. We will share." The young Arab stood up and limped over to a stone counter. His leg was twisted so that the foot faced the wrong way. "I am the *mukhtar,* the mayor."

"I am the Messiah," Pirkl said.

There was a small fishbowl in the middle of the table. A single goldfish swam in a few inches of murky water.

"I am really the *mukhtar*," he said, handing Pirkl a glass of water. He had a sparse mustache, and his eyes wandered lazily. The goldfish swam rapidly back and forth.

"A Jewish fish," he said. "A gefilte fish," he added, laughing.

Pirkl drank the water, thankful but annoyed by the young Arab.

"Can you keep a secret?" he said, spitting a date pit onto the ground. Pirkl nodded.

"This fish. He does not belong to me. It is the only gold I got from the houses. Who has ever seen a fish in the desert?"

Pirkl thanked him for the water and stood up to leave.

"Wait, wait," the young Arab said, his eyes looking past Pirkl. "I want to show you something." He stood up and clubbed his way over to a cabinet, returning with a pile of photographs. He smiled. "Look. Jews!"

Pirkl saw mutilated bodies, both male and female, their faces twisted, smashed, eyeless. Disemboweled bodies, here he saw an arm, there a leg, and wondered if he would recognize his father's hand among those bodies. A bare bootless foot, burned and bloody. Would he know?

Pirkl leaned over and heaved onto the ground. Only the water came out, clear and hot. He coughed and coughed and finally stood up. "I'm going."

"Wait, wait," the young Arab said. "Please. Take the fish. He does not belong to me."

Pirkl grabbed the tiny fishbowl in his arms and ran up

the cobbled street toward the once glorious Tiferet Israel Synagogue.

"Careful," the Arab called after him. "Don't spill."

On the next street a half-dozen fierce-looking irregulars from the Liberation Army ransacked a house. Pirkl hid behind a wall as the men cut open a mattress in search of treasure, laughing as the stuffing flew out. One man wearing a British-style helmet fired his rifle into the mattress.

Pirkl turned up a narrow alley, the blanket almost totally obscuring his face. The two mortar shells clinked together as he walked. Then he heard it, at first one voice, then hundreds, singing, he was sure he heard singing: the Shema. He ran toward the voices that seemed to be coming from out of the stones themselves. "Hear, O Israel: the Lord our God. The Lord is one!" He ran as fast as he could without spilling the goldfish onto the maze-like streets.

He arrived at Ashkenazi Square dazed, but exhilarated by the sound of the voices. Hundreds of people milled about; men with beards and sidecurls, wide-brimmed felt hats and long coats, carrying bundles in their arms; women wearing babushkas and long dresses stared blankly; boys in shorts and sandals and pigtailed girls huddled close to their parents, scratching at the earth with their feet.

The dome of Tiferet Israel seemed to have been erased, supplanted only by the blue sky. All the windows were blown out and bullet holes peppered the walls. Pirkl pulled the blanket off his head as he noticed kaffiyeh-wearing men, with bandoliers slung across their chests, standing close by with rifles in their arms. He wandered confused through the crowd with the goldfish bowl in his arms.

"It's over," a man in beige pants and shirt said in English, walking through the crowd. "It's all over. Your rabbis are in the Armenian Seminary now discussing the terms of the surrender." The letters "U.N." were painted in white on his helmet.

Surrender! Over! Pirkl thought. What is over? It can't be. We still have my two mortars. We're not done yet. I have bullets. I'll fight. It can't be over. The Old City is over?

Most of the men were Orthodox Jews who would not have picked up a gun to fight.

"Where are the fighters?" Pirkl asked a man swaying, lost in prayer. "Where is my father?" he asked another, who said something in Yiddish. "Why didn't you fight instead of pray?" he said to another, kicking dust up at him.

He saw a young girl standing alone on the edge of the crowd staring into the distance. She reminded him of Hannah the way her shoulder blades showed through the back of her dress, the way her hair was cut unevenly at the neck. He touched her arm softly and held out the goldfish to the girl.

"Does this fish belong to you?"

She looked through him as if he were not there and batted the fishbowl out of his hands. It shattered on the ground. Watching the fish struggle for a last breath of desert air, Pirkl wanted to cry, but he did not want his father to see him crying like a baby.

"You are looking for the *Portzim?*" a man asked Pirkl. "Go to Rothschild House."

Pirkl went. And there he found more refugees gathering baskets and bedding onto their shoulders. One woman carried a baby in her arms and a box of matzo. He saw a crowd of men standing beneath the arches of Rothschild House, soldiers in beige short-sleeved shirts, some wearing wool caps, others bareheaded, exhausted, weary, standing with their hands at their sides. There were no more than two dozen of them and Pirkl scanned their faces. And then he saw his father standing with a coat slung coolly over his shoulder. Pirkl ran to him, threw his arms around his father's waist.

"Malchyk! What are you doing here?" his father asked, disentangling Pirkl from his waist. "Where's your mother?"

"Look what I brought," Pirkl said, opening his satchel. "We're not beat yet!"

"Go back to the square. Get out of here."

The harshness of his father's voice broke Pirkl's heart. He had never heard him speak that way, and he burst into tears, throwing a bear hug around his father's waist.

"Look! I brought bullets."

"I want you to go back home," his father said.

"But, we still have my shells."

"Why didn't you stay with your mother?" his father said, shaking his head.

Pirkl knew he couldn't go home now, he wasn't a quitter. He stood in silence next to his father, writing his name in the dusty earth with his foot.

A few minutes later a smartly dressed Arab Legion officer addressed the group of assembled soldiers in both English and Arabic. "From this moment on, you are prisoners of His Majesty King Abdullah of Transjordan and you cannot be harmed."

. . .

The prisoners were marched along the Gate of Heaven Road toward the old Turkish prison near Jaffa Gate. Pirkl felt his legs were too short as he walked behind his father, who did not say a word, or look back. One of the fighters put his Haganah cap on Pirkl's head as they filed along Rehov Beit El, House of the Lord Street, and asked him his name. He said only his last name. The fighter tapped Pirkl's father on the shoulder and said, "The youth brigade has taken over." Before turning up Rehov Ha Yehudim, the Street of the Jews, Pirkl's father finally did look around and he saw his downcast young son and the Jewish Quarter burning at their backs.

From the prison window as he tried to sleep, Pirkl could see the Tower of David rising from the Citadel. He imagined climbing the stone walls of the tower, wrapping his arms around its neck and reaching out for the moon, hovering low over the blanched city; and there were no fires, and there was no bombing, only the scattered sky filled with stars and the lonely tooting of a single shepherd's flute. Pirkl did not know then that he would spend the next half year in a Jordanian prison camp where he would sleep in a tent beneath a cold moon and become bar mitzvah in the Iraqi desert. He did not know that he would not return to the Old City until another nineteen years and another war had passed, and that he would enter Lion's Gate as a soldier, only footsteps behind the future prime minister. He did not know as he knelt by the prison window that his mother searched hospitals and makeshift infirmaries for her only son. He imagined his mother standing on the rooftop of their apartment house in Rehavia sadly looking toward the walled city. And he called to her and waved his free arm and said, "Momma, I found him. I found him!"

An Unwelcome
Guest

YOSSI BAR-YOSEF FELT his young wife Devorah stir in sleep. He rolled over in bed, felt her warm breath against his face and lay watching her until she was still again. Then she slept quietly. A large round moon hung low over Jerusalem, its white light spilling into their Muslim Quarter apartment. He sat up in bed, reached for his *kippah* on the nightstand, and placed it on his head. The night was silent in contrast to the chaos of the day; Arab merchants hawking fruits and vegetables, pilgrims shouting prayers and curses, army patrols strolling through the narrow stone streets. Now he could only hear his wife's even breathing and the two soldiers joking quietly in Hebrew beneath their bedroom window. In a few hours the muezzin would call the Ishmaelites to prayer for the first time in the new day.

He got out of bed and made his way to the kitchen by moonlight, nearly skipping all the way in his bare feet. It was the month of Tishri and the stone floors were chilly even for early autumn. He filled a pot with water, lit the gas with a match, and stood by the stove for a moment thinking of his wife, his Devorah Bee: her soft olive skin, her curly brown hair, her green eyes, the way her body felt beneath his.

"You are welcome," the Arab man said, startling Yossi. "Welcome. Have a seat," he said gesturing to the empty chair at the kitchen table. "Welcome," the Arab man said again, smiling.

Yossi did not wonder how the old man had crept past

the soldiers in the street, nor did he wonder how he had found his way through the locked door. He had waited every Passover for Elijah the Prophet to arrive and drink his cup of wine, and he prayed daily for the coming of the Messiah. Yossi knew that many people wandered the dreamy moonlit paths between sleep and prayer in this golden city of light and stone.

The Arab may have been sixty-five or seventy years old. His face was cracked like a wadi in the heat of summer, his nose round, bulbous, and pocked like a Judean hilltop, his thin salt and pepper mustache ratty, careless, a goatherd's mustache. He wore a black and white checked kaffiyeh on his head and a filthy striped caftan that reached almost to his slippered feet.

"Sit," said the Arab man in English. "We will share some tea and nana."

"What do you want here?"

The Arab man said nothing.

"My wife. She's sleeping."

"She sleeps like a baby."

The thought of someone invading his new wife's privacy, someone even imagining Devorah asleep infuriated Yossi. He took a step forward and whispered through his teeth, "Get out! Why are you —"

"The water is ready," the Arab man said, cutting Yossi off.

Yossi turned his attention to the pot. The water bubbled over, hissing against the stove's flames.

"My name is Ziad."

"Who *are* you?" Yossi asked.

"I am Ziad Abu Youssif."

"You are in the wrong place. This is a private home," Yossi said, returning with the pot of water.

The old man only straightened his kaffiyeh on his head, smiled, and reached for a glass. He poured himself some water and said, "You are a rabbi?"

"No. No. I am studying. Near the Kotel."

The Arab man smiled a brown-toothed smile. "So you are a rabbi."

"I'm not a rabbi yet. I am studying," Yossi said, and then asked, "Why are you here?"

"This is my home, rabbi," the Arab man answered in an even tone. "A tea bag, please."

"Your home?" Yossi said, surprised. "This is *my* home."

"How long have you stayed here?" the Arab man asked.

"Eight months."

"You are just married?" the Arab asked, taking a tea bag from a tin on the table. "Where are you from?"

"New York," Yossi answered.

"I was born in that room, where you sleep. My first son, Youssif, the dark one, was born in the same room. My father was born where you are sitting. This was not always a kitchen."

"If this is your house what color are the tiles on the floor of my bedroom?"

"The Jews are always changing things."

They sat in silence while their tea brewed in front of them. Then they drank. After a moment Yossi bit his lip at the corner, about to ask, "Why did you leave?" but before he had a chance, the old man said, "There were wars."

Yossi knew that many Arabs had fled Israel in 1948 and again during the Six-Day War. He had seen the squalid refugee camps and the anguished faces on his TV set, but he also knew the names Chmelnicki, Babi-Yar, and Auschwitz like a mantra. After a moment he said, "Abraham is your father as well as mine."

The old man did not seem to hear as he bent over to pick something up off the floor. It was a small wooden box. The Arab carefully placed it on the table between them. Yossi swallowed hard and thought about calling to the soldiers outside the window, but knew it would be useless. The bomb would go off before they could make it halfway up the stairs.

It had only been eight months since he and Devorah had stood under the *huppa,* only eight months since he had first kissed her after stomping the traditional glass representing the fragility of life, eight months since he had first touched his virgin wife. That was supposed to be the beginning; a family, a Jewish family in the heart of Jerusalem, and now, they were about to be blown to bits like that bus he had seen smoldering in the spring rain on Jaffa Street.

The Arab man undid a small latch and folded open a backgammon board.

"You play *shesh besh*?" he asked.

Yossi looked out the window and could see the moon higher over the city now, its light so bright, the face of the moon almost pulsing.

"It's the middle of the night."

The Arab began setting up the board, the white stones first, then the black stone disks in their places.

The old man took the last sip of his tea. "I will play you for the house. If you lose, I will live here again. If I lose, I will return to the Street of Chains begging for baksheesh."

Yossi was not interested in hearing about a broken man begging for shekels. He said, "No," and then said, "no," again.

"I am joking, of course," the Arab man said. "We will play for the right to speak."

Yossi would not get back to sleep now. He could feel his blood boiling through his body, his hands shaking, the small hairs at the back of his neck standing on end. "Okay. I'll play. Just let me check on my wife."

"But, it's your turn to roll." The Arab man had already rolled the first die: a four.

Yossi imagined his Devorah Bee curled up in bed, wetting her lips in sleep, kicking her leg against a bad dream. He thought of her slightly rounded belly and the child swimming within it. He stood halfway up from his chair, then picked up the die and rolled a three.

"My move first," the Arab man said. "Some more tea."

The old man rolled a six and a one. He moved the black stone to his side of the outer board, covering it with the one. Yossi rolled a two and a one. Already, one of his stones was unprotected. The Arab picked up the dice in his large hands and rolled. Then Yossi rolled. Only the sound of the dice clicking against the wooden board could be heard above the old man's labored breathing.

"Do you speak Hebrew?" the Arab asked.

"To read the Torah," Yossi answered, head down.

"Tell me, Rabbi, how did you get here?"

Yossi tried to move his two white stones from the inner board but could not. His pieces were almost entirely blocked in.

"Why here?" the Arab said.

"'If I should forget thee, O Jerusalem, may my right hand forget its strength.' *Tehillim*. Psalm One thirty-seven," Yossi said.

"I do not forget," the Arab man said, holding out his right hand.

Yossi did not look up from the board and said matter-of-factly, "This land was given to Abraham by God. Abraham was the father of the Jews. We are here because we are Jewish. Because the land was promised to us by God."

The Arab rolled again, saying, "But we are both sons of Abraham."

Yossi rolled quickly and made his move. His mind was not on the game now. The Arab rolled the dice again.

"Abraham was the best of men," Yossi continued flatly, "but he contained some bad elements as we all do and those elements came out in his son Ishmael. He was the son of a slave girl. A wild man."

The old man's stones were all strongly in place on his side of the inner board. Yossi rolled but still could not move his two white stones trapped deep among the Arab's black stones. The Arab rolled and began removing his pieces from the board. "Beit 'Itab," he whispered. "Beit Mahsir," he said on his next roll. "Deir el Hawa," he said, removing two more pieces. "Jarash." "Lifta." "El Maliha." "Suba," he said, winning the game. Yossi cleared the board and began to set up another game.

"Deir Yassin!" the Arab said loudly. "Do you know Deir Yassin, Rabbi?"

Yossi motioned for the man to be quiet, he did not want to wake up his wife. The Arab lowered his voice.

"Do you know of Deir Yassin? No. It was a beautiful little village of orange and lemon trees, almond trees, and date palms on the outside of Jerusalem. Like the others, it is also erased from the face of the earth. Now it is called Givat Shaul. I'm sure you know Givat Shaul."

He did know Givat Shaul; his wife's aunt and uncle lived in an apartment not far from the mental institution. He had visited once or twice, but never saw a sign of Deir Yassin.

"You came to Deir Yassin one morning —"

Yossi interrupted, "I've never been —"

"It's my time to speak. I won the game. Now you must listen."

Yossi shifted uncomfortably in his chair.

"You came to Deir Yassin, a small quiet village at dawn. You were three hundred men with guns and mortars. You broke into homes, shot whole families, women and children, threw bombs into houses, machine-gunned us, butchered us, raped us. You took prisoners into the streets blindfolded and shot us dead. You left our bodies on the ground. You bound our hands, stripped us naked, put us in trucks, and drove us through the streets of Jerusalem. We were afraid and some of us ran."

Nonsense! Yossi thought. He had not even received his military training yet. He rolled the wooden die.

"You tried to scare the Arabs out of Jerusalem," the old man said and straightened his kaffiyeh. Then he rolled a three. It was Yossi's turn to roll first. The moon had moved behind some clouds, leaving them in almost complete darkness.

"Do you have a candle?" the old man asked.

Yossi stood up in silence, walked to the pantry, and returned with two Shabbat candles. He lit them.

"We'll play until the winner of three," the Arab said.

This time Yossi was determined not to get caught in the back of the board. He would rush his two white stones out from the very start and race the rest of his stones around to his side before the Arab could do the same. Yossi rolled, and then the old man, and then Yossi. They moved quickly, sliding their stones around the board, hypnotized by the rhythm of the rolling dice. He was so busy concentrating on the board that he did not notice the old man had been speaking in Arabic. Smelling tobacco smoke, Yossi looked up from the table to find three more Arab men sitting on the kitchen floor beside the old man. He grabbed the table, nearly knocking the board to the floor as he tried to stand up. But he was unable, paralyzed in his seat. Two men slightly younger than Ziad wore kaffiyehs and took turns smoking from a tall gold-plated water pipe, a third ancient man with a battered fez planted on his head awkwardly fingered a set of worry beads. Yossi could still hear the soldiers' radio crackling faintly outside his kitchen window.

"Do not worry," Ziad said. "We are old men. There is nothing to fear. They are only my brothers and our blind father. Do not worry. Please. Please play."

The four men continued to talk in Arabic. Yossi, not understanding Arabic, did not know what to do. He took a deep breath but still could not fill his lungs.

Ziad asked Yossi, "Do you smoke the nargilah?"

"No. No," Yossi said, coughing. Then he remembered his pregnant wife as smoke filled the kitchen. Yossi excused himself.

From the bedroom doorway he saw Devorah asleep as before, her long hair splashed out onto the pillow. Yossi sat on the bed for a moment looking at her. Moonlight shined through the window and lit up her face. He kissed his index finger and touched it to the end of her nose. "Sleep tight, my Bumblebee," he whispered and opened her night table drawer, removed his wife's mini 9 mm pistol, and placed it in his side pocket. Then he closed the bedroom door tight and hurried back to the kitchen half afraid of the encroaching Arabs, half determined to prove that he could win the game.

"She is sleeping?" Ziad asked.

Yossi nodded his head and sat down at the table.

"I shared that room with my brothers as a child," the old man said.

Yossi rolled the dice, ignoring him.

"There was a pomegranate tree at the window. My son Youssif liked to climb in it."

"It isn't there anymore," Yossi said, rolling a three and a one. He moved his first lone stone four spaces and said, "The tree is gone. There is no tree."

"I am just remembering," the old man said.

Yossi's white stone was open at the edge of the outer board one space short of safety. The old man paused a long time before rolling the dice again. With the moon high above the apartment the three Arabs sat cross-legged on the floor; two of them passing the water pipe back and forth between them, the older man continuing to fumble with his worry beads. It was only now with the moon out of the clouds that Yossi noticed the blind father's empty eye sockets.

"How would you feel if someone took that glass of tea from you?" Ziad asked.

"This glass?" Yossi said.

"Yes. That glass," the Arab said, rolling the dice.

"I would get another glass."

The old man rolled and promptly hit Yossi's single stone, removing it to the center bar. Yossi rolled, and entered in the fourth slot, moving his other lone piece from the first to third slot. His two stones were now open at the back end of the board. The Arab rolled again and Yossi found his stone back on the bar with the fourth and sixth slots occupied. He rolled a two and a three. His stone came off the center bar, but Yossi's stones were still hemmed in.

The Arab asked, "How old is your wife, Rabbi?"

"Nineteen," Yossi answered.

"And what is her name?" the Arab asked, rolling and knocking Yossi's stone to the bar again.

Yossi did not answer.

The game continued, and Yossi's stones were alternately knocked onto the center bar as the old man removed his pieces from the table two by two, whispering in Arabic. The Arab men on the floor clapped their hands on each other's shoulders — the blind old man mumbled something in Arabic that could have been a prayer.

"I've had enough of this. I'm going to sleep," Yossi said. He had not removed any of his stones from the table.

"But you can't. Nobody has won three games. Sit. Sit. I won the second game."

One of the Arab men got to his feet, a silver sheath shining among the folds of his caftan. Yossi fingered his wife's pistol in his pocket and said, "Okay. We'll play another game."

The old man picked up the stones in his hands and began chanting quietly the names he had just whispered: "'Allar;

'Artuf; Beit Naqquba; Deir Aban; Ishwa'; El Jura; Kasla!" Do you know of the village of —"

"All right. It's time to play," Yossi said.

Yossi began setting up the board.

They played on, the dice rattling against the old wooden board. The men on the floor were anxious, groaning in discomfort with every move, shifting from one knee to the other. Yossi blocked the men from his mind, focusing only on the board. When he had established a lead he looked and flashed a confident wink at Ziad. The old man sat calmly, pondering his next move. Then he called out a question in Arabic and was answered by a woman's voice.

Four Arab women dressed in black stood over the kneeling men. One wore a *hijab* over her face, the other three sternly looked on. One of the women spoke loudly in guttural Arabic. The old man listened and turned to Yossi, who was beginning to remove his stones from the board.

"My wife, Zahira," Ziad said.

Yossi continued to play, ignoring her. His only interest now was to beat the old man, throw the Arabs from his home, and return to bed with his wife.

"These are my brothers' wives. And," he said, pointing to the tiny woman in the *hijab,* "this is our mother."

"It's your move," Yossi said.

The old man rolled. He had twelve stones left on the board. Yossi had six and rolled low but still removed two stones. The woman who had spoken to Ziad pushed her way forward and placed her hands on the table. Yossi saw the black under her fingernails, her eyes cold as the chipped stones on the board. Her face had the worn look of an old leather saddle. He rolled double four and won the game. The woman grabbed up the pieces and began to quickly reset the board. Yossi tried to place his hand on top of hers. She pulled away.

"Hevron!" he said, making eye contact with all the Arabs except the blind father. "We were neighbors in Hevron and you came to our homes," Yossi said, borrowing the tone of the old man, Ziad. "And you raped us, burned us, chopped off our hands."

"That is not true," the woman said.

"It is true," Yossi said.

"Liar!" the woman said louder.

"You were not born then," Ziad said.

"You came to our homes in the City of the Patriarchs —" Yossi said.

"Isra-ay-lee pig!" the woman yelled. "Liar!"

"— and tore us apart like fresh bread," he added.

"Arrogant Jew. Liar. Zionist," the woman shouted, and the men joined in shouting, knocking against the table. The woman stood face to face with Yossi and said, "You have no place here. Pig!" Then she spat in his face.

Yossi reached into his side pocket, pulled out his wife's pistol, and jammed it hard beneath the woman's ribs, doubling her over momentarily. He felt her soft stomach rebound against his hand.

"Quiet!"

The men moved back, but Zahira, the wife of the old man Ziad, stood her ground. "Put your toy away, *yeled*."

"It was a long time ago," the old man said.

"It was only sixty years ago," Yossi said.

"You were not born. You were not there," the old man said.

"Memory is in the blood," Yossi said. "I was there as I

was at Sinai to receive the commandments. I was exiled from Spain. I wandered. And I remember pogroms beyond the Pale and the killing. I remember. And the camps, I remember that, too. Jews have been in Hevron since the time of Abraham. You have only lived there since the thirteenth century."

He waved the pistol at the Arabs and tasted blood in his mouth, sour and metallic. He wanted to lay the Arabs face down on the floor with their hands behind their backs, and fire a bullet into the brain of each. He would clean the floor with the old man's kaffiyeh and return to bed with his wife.

Zahira stepped closer, her weathered face inches from his. "Okay, boy," she said. "Shoot me." She pulled his pistol closer to her stomach. Yossi's hand was compliant. "I am all used up," she said. "Make me a martyr of the great battle." The men looked on impassively, the women stood stone-faced. Ziad, too, stared expressionless. "I am the mother of generations. But now I am finished. I am the husk of a pome-granate, my seeds have been scattered and grown. Shoot me. I am only a husk." Yossi pushed his pistol into her stomach and then pulled it back.

"Sit. We're going to play again," Yossi said.

The men sat, and the women did too.

Zahira reached forward and touched Yossi's cheek and said, "You are weak and sad."

"We will play?" Ziad said.

"Do not fear us," Zahira said. "We are old and not to be feared. But fear our children. Fear my son Youssif. He will burn your crops, tear down your home, and eat the flesh of your children."

Yossi rolled the dice.

"He will eat the flesh of your children," she repeated.

They began to play again, the Arab leading two games to one. The sky was turning from deep black to dark bruised blue. The moon was gone. Yossi slipped the pistol back into his pocket.

"The tea. It is cold," the old man said.

Yossi stood up to boil another pot of water, then returned to his seat and rolled the dice. He opened with a solid four and two, occupying the four slot on the inner table.

"My sweet wife was beautiful as a flower," Ziad said. "We married when she was fifteen. Her lovely name means flowers."

The old man rolled and Yossi turned to the woman.

"I brought her to the place to take her gift, and my father and uncles waited outside the room with stones and knives — if she was not a virgin. But there was blood. . . ."

Yossi remembered his wife's red blood on the white bedsheet and the feeling that she was truly his.

"It hurt her and she cried and cried for days, did not stop."

Yossi rolled again.

"And we prayed that, *Inshallah,* we would have a strong boy who would not cry," Zahira, the old man's wife, said.

"And when he was born he cried," the old man said. "He cried for Palestine, and the bloodstained hilltops, and the weeping seashores. And I slapped his face and shook him and said, 'Do not be weak! You are an Arab!' And Youssif grew to be an angry barefoot boy."

The old man rolled and Yossi watched him slide the stones around the board with his rough fingers. The smell of hashish mixed with the smell of tobacco filled the room. Yossi was afraid to look up, feeling the weight of claustrophobia on him. He just stared at the board and at the old man's chipped black stones.

"It's your turn," the old man said.

The room was jammed with Arabs. The children had arrived. Eight young men with thick hair and mustaches crowded around the table with the others. Yossi could feel one of the newcomers breathing at his neck. Some drank beer from brown bottles, others smoked. They were all slim and strong and Yossi was afraid. The kitchen was so crowded that the Arabs pressed right up against the table and chairs.

"I need room," Yossi said and the woman called out, "Lebensraum?" and laughed. "I need room," Yossi said again, but the Arabs either could not or would not move. Then he thought of his wife alone in the bedroom and wanted to run to her.

"It's your turn," the old man said. Yossi stared blank-faced. "My sons," the old man said. "And my brothers' sons."

"I don't want to play."

"But you must. We are the majority," the Arab said.

Yossi wanted to call the soldiers down below, but couldn't raise his voice to speak. His wife's pistol in his pocket comforted him, but he knew he would never use it. He rolled again. Then the old man rolled. The young Arabs pressing in toward the table kept a running commentary of the game in Arabic. One imitated the sound of the clicking dice with his tongue. Yossi rolled again and he was leading. He removed his first stone from the board. The old man held up his empty cup and said, "Your pot is burning." Black smoke rose from the stove.

"Your house is on fire," the woman said.

Yossi pushed his chair back into one of the Arabs, stood

up and forced his way to the stove. The Arabs laughed, and as he waded through them and tried to pull his *kippah* from his head, one reached into his pocket. Someone had thrown a dish towel into the flame. Yossi dropped it into the sink with the blackened pot and turned on the water.

"Some more tea," the old man said in a cracking voice.

When Yossi returned to the table his white stone was on the bar and six or seven of the Arab's stones had been spirited away without even a single roll of the dice.

"Where is the tea?" the old man asked.

"There is no tea," Yossi said. "Put the stones back or I won't play."

"All right. I will put them back and you will play."

"Where is your toy?" the woman asked.

Yossi felt his side pocket. His wife's pistol was gone and had been replaced with a slab of olive wood. Yossi's head felt light and then heavy.

"You will play now," the old man said.

Yossi's stomach churned and his mouth tasted bitter, acidy. With the pieces back in place, he rolled again, more determined than ever to beat the Arabs. "When I win you'll give me back my gun," Yossi said.

"You still don't understand. We make the rules," the old man said.

Yossi bit his lip and rolled again — double four. A lucky roll. Five stones left. The room still smelled of hashish now mixed with body odor and Yossi's head felt too heavy for his neck. The Arabs rolled. Then Yossi — two more stones off the board.

"Which one is Youssif?" Yossi asked.

The young Arabs laughed and one called out, "Youssif no home."

"Youssif is not here yet," the old man said.

Yossi put his hand to his forehead and rolled again — two more stones.

"You have won," the old man said, picking the last stone off the board with his battered fingers. "Now tell me of the six million, or some other lies, Rabbi."

"Tell me, Jew," the woman said. "Tell me some more fairy stories."

Yossi remembered the burned-out carcass of the bus on Jaffa Street, the shattered glass, the body parts scattered in the street. The bomb blast had woken him and Devorah in their apartment within the walls of the Old City. He had rushed from their bedroom to see, arriving while the acrid smell of burning flesh was still thick in the air.

"Bus number eighteen. I was there when the second bus blew up."

"Good. We have a bomb-maker here," the woman said, pronouncing the second "b" as she pointed to the young Arabs.

"He's a terrorist and should be killed," Yossi said, remembering the *Hesed shel Emet* workers cleaning flesh from the statue of the winged lion who sat perched atop the Generali Building.

"That is not very humane. Does your Torah allow that, Rabbi?" the old man said, setting up the board.

"The Torah of Israel is not about being humane," Yossi said. "This is the land of Isaac and Jacob. This is the land of my fathers and the land of my children and it will be the land of their children. This is our land. The land of Israel. The land of the Jewish people. I don't give a damn about your orange trees and date palms and pomegranate trees. You do not belong here. You are Amalek. I should have poisoned your tea."

"You should have," the old man said. "But your right hand forgot its strength."

"What?" Yossi said, stunned.

"I have read your books, Rabbi. Does it not say, if someone is going to kill you, it is your duty to rise early and kill him first? Yes, I am Amalek and you are not welcome here. You have scattered my children, chopped down my trees, thrown me from my home," the Arab said. "I am a son of Ishmael and you are a son of Isaac. But for that, we are not enemies. We are enemies because you came to make a family in Al-Quds. The land of Palestine is an Islamic holy possession, given to future Muslims until Judgment Day. You are a cancer and you must be cut out." The Arab paused for a moment. "Now it is your turn to roll again."

Before Yossi had a chance to reply, he heard what sounded like a window smashing in his wife's room, the glass shattering onto the stone floor. Yossi's stomach turned. He tried to stand up but was forced down by his shoulders.

"Help!" he called, before the old man pulled off his checked kaffiyeh and stuffed it into Yossi's mouth with the help of his laughing nephews.

"If I forget thee, let my tongue cleave to the roof of my mouth," the old man said, shaking his head.

"Psalm One thirty-seven," Yossi thought, sickened.

Yossi could hear someone stepping through the broken glass. His wife, in a panic, would rise in search of her gun, pull open her night table drawer and find it empty. The taste of the dirty kaffiyeh in his mouth made Yossi want to throw up.

"*Hacol b'seder?*" a soldier called from beneath the kitchen window.

"*B'seder,*" one of the Arabs answered.

"*Lo b'seder,*" Yossi thought in Hebrew. "It's not okay. There are Arabs in my kitchen!"

"*Tov,*" the soldier said. Then there was silence.

The old man placed the dice in Yossi's hand. He dropped them onto the board.

"A good roll," the old man said, moving Yossi's pieces around the table. "Do you have *mazel* tonight?" the Arab man said mockingly.

The sky outside the window was turning quickly from a deep blue to a glowing purple. The bald old man reached into his caftan, removed Devorah Bee's mini 9 mm pistol and placed it on the table. Yossi struggled but could not move. He was held in place by three of the young Arabs. "My children studied at the revolutionary school. They drank anger and ate fury and threw stones. But they are not just bomb-makers and pickpockets. They will be the leaders of this land." The old man prodded the pistol with his index finger and spun it on the board. There was an inscription on the handle.

"What's this?" the old man said, "'DARLING DEVORAH: FOR A SAFE LIFE IN JERUSALEM. LOVE DADDY.' A thoughtful gift, and practical, may it protect her from all harm. And a very pretty name. What does Devorah mean?"

Yossi blinked his eyes hard and fast as if he were trying to say, "Fuck you. Fuck your mother you filthy Arab."

The woman picked up the gun and held it against Yossi's

temple. Then she pulled his *kippah* from his head and dropped it to the floor. "It is almost time to pray," she said.

Yossi prayed to his God, wishing Moses had never led his people out of the wilderness, wishing that he had never come to this violent desert land, wishing that he and Devorah were safe in bed back in New York.

The old man looked on, his big eyes pitying, his pink peeling head almost glowing as the sun continued to rise.

Yossi looked at the woman, her face as hard as fire-forged steel. And then the muezzin cried, calling the Arabs to prayer. *"Ull-aaaaaaw-hoo-Ak-bar! Ull-aaaaaaw-hoo-Ak-bar!"* And the unwelcome guests, as surprisingly as they had arrived, began disappearing into the blue morning light. The blind father, the wives, the mother, the woman, the sons, and the nephews dropped to their knees, foreheads on the floor. And were gone. The old man, too, climbed from his chair and vanished. Yossi pulled the dirty kaffiyeh from his mouth and ran to the hallway, his heart breaking in his throat. The bedroom door opened and out stepped Youssif, a tall handsome Arab in a sweater and slacks. He held a broken bottle in his hand.

Youssif stepped past him, dropping the bloodied bottle to the floor.

"She is not dead," Youssif said. "She is only crying for the ghosts of her children and their children, too."

The sun continued to rise, the muezzin wailing in Arabic, "There is no God but Allah and Muhammad is the messenger of Allah."

The Art of
Correcting

ONE MORNING, Rabbi Israel Frummann could not rise from his bed to say his morning prayers. It was the first time in his entire sixty-three years that the great Dokszycer rebbe did not greet the new day with prayer on his lips.

"My back is aching," he said to his wife, Sarah. "I can't move."

"Get up. You must go and pray."

"Like the mortar of Egypt," he cried. "I am turning to stone."

She brought him a hot towel to lie on and some ointment for his neck. He waved it away and then winced.

"All right, my wife. Bring it here."

"Then you must go and pray. You are the rebbe."

With that, the Dokszycer rebbe pulled himself up on his elbows and then fell quickly back onto his pillows. "I cannot go," he said.

"But what about the minyan?" Sarah said, raising her voice.

The Dokszycer sect was a very small order, so small in fact that without the rebbe, only nine men could appear at the Western Wall to perform morning prayers.

"Don't worry, they can worship without me," the rebbe said. "They are all grown men."

"What do you mean?" Sarah said, horrified. "Man's prayers are only truly heard when he prays as part of a congregation. Get out of bed now!"

"All right, wife," the rebbe said and began resolutely to climb from his bed, but screamed out in pain, "The Angel of Death is killing me slowly."

"Are you going to pray?" Sarah said.

"His sword is wedged in my spine!"

"Then, rest," Sarah said, finally. "I will bring you some tea and honey."

"Bring me Luria!"

Lev Luria was a local kabbalist whose mastery of amulets, prayers, and spells was known outside Jerusalem as far as Bnei Brak. It was said he had once revived a dead yeshiva student who had been hit by a bus simply by breathing the word *chayim,* life, into his mouth.

Pale, long-faced Luria arrived sometime after noon and found the rebbe in bed with his window curtains pulled closed.

"The rebbitzin sent for me. What is the matter?" Luria said, stepping close to the rebbe's bed.

"I did not go to prayers this morning," the rebbe said in such a sad tone that he may have been lying on his death bed.

"Why me?" Luria asked, placing his hands in his pockets and stepping away.

"My back feels like it has been walked on by an elephant. My spine has been a ladder for a thousand monkeys. . . ."

Luria took a step closer to the bed. The rebbe was not dying. "How are your eyes?"

"My eyes?" the rebbe said, trying to lift his head from the flattened pillow. "They hurt sometimes."

"It is not your back," Luria said, and a thin smile formed on his face. "The Talmud says a heavy step detracts one five-hundredth from the light of your eyes. Rebbe, if I may be so bold, there is nothing wrong with your back. You must simply learn to take lighter steps or else" — and here Luria's voice fell to a whisper — "you will be blind before the year is over."

"What shall I do?" the rebbe asked.

"Tomorrow you will walk. But softly. Today we must take care of your precious eyes."

"Yes. Yes! We must. Without my eyes I cannot read the Torah."

Lev Luria concocted a potion of kiddush wine, sage, egg yolk, and a sprinkle of golden Jerusalem earth to bathe the eyes of the ailing rebbe. He also placed a fist-sized stone, purplish-blue in color, underneath the rebbe's mattress.

"This is the Stone of Issachar. It will help cure what ails you."

Sarah applied the concoction to the eyelids of her husband, and stroked his hair when she was done. Then, she placed two cucumber slices on his eyes and told him to rest.

The next day, the rebbe was in a rage. He had slept badly, tossing and turning from the pain, feeling every contour of the Stone of Issachar beneath his back. And now his eyes really did hurt. They were red and bloodshot, and he screamed at his wife Sarah to call the kabbalist to come to his bedside immediately.

"What's the matter?" Luria said, entering the dark room shortly afterwards. He leaned over and pulled back the rebbe's eyelids with his index fingers.

"Worse today," the rebbe moaned.

"Good, we have no time to waste. It is happening even faster than I thought. You must stand up now."

"But I can't," the rebbe said. "Termites are eating at me."

"Stand up," Luria said, and pulled the rebbe's arm.

The rebbe slid out of bed and fell onto the floor in a heap of bones. He felt as if he was going to burst into flames. "Pick me up," he screamed.

"The floor is hard. Today you will sleep on the floor."

The great Dokszycer rebbe cried out for his wife Sarah to throw the mad kabbalist from his house. "The Dokszycer rebbe does not sleep on the floor. My father slept on goose-down, and his father on swan feathers."

That evening, the rebbe's followers stood above him and performed the *Ma'ariv* services. From the floor the rebbe could easily see the nine smiling faces that completed the minyan. He slept better that evening, but in the morning, cried out in pain once again.

Sarah came to comfort him with a cold towel for his forehead, and though she was not much taller than his congregation's large Torah scroll, he believed she could cure any ill. "If I see that Luria again, I will beat him about the head," Sarah said, shaking her little fist like a dried-out citron. "He is as bad as the cut-and-slash doctors. I will fix you a warm bath with Epsom salts."

"Wife," the rebbe said, "how wonderful it would be to pray again at the Wall and to walk back and forth over the earth as I please. But I am afraid my spine is broken like a matchstick."

Sarah knelt down and he looked into her smooth, worn face and remembered her as a young girl when she still wore braids on either side of her head. Now she wore a blue snood adorned with gold stars that covered all of her still-brown hair. "You are a good wife. Bring me the bottle of wine."

Sarah brought an herbalist who concocted a mixture of valerian root, skullcap, and devil's claw to soothe the rebbe's pains, but the rebbe wouldn't touch the murky elixir and shouted the herbalist from his home. Sarah brought a Yemenite master of prayer who offered mud and salts from the Dead Sea to rub against his skin, and a rabbi who could read cures in the stars, but the rebbe would not see them, preferring the solitude of his dark room. Sarah only entered while he slept to remove the refuse bucket from beside the bed. When she brought him food and knocked, saying, "If you chew well with your teeth, your back will find its strength," he said he was not hungry. When she said, "You must drink," he called out, "More wine!"

Finally, the rebbe called Sarah to open the door. She entered, and the dark room smelled stale and musty like old books and bedsheets. The rebbe lay on the bed with pillows propped under his legs and back.

"How does one begin a conversation with God?" the rebbe began, his voice thin and strained. "How does one start such a conversation? What does one say?"

"You are tired," Sarah said.

"What does one say? And in what language?" the rebbe said.

"You know what to do," Sarah said.

"I have never had such a conversation."

The rebbe lived every day in the shadow of his great-great-grandfather, the first Dokszycer rebbe, peace be upon him, who had summoned God to protect his village from rampaging cossacks. It is said that he stood in the village square with his eyes closed as cossack hoofbeats pounded nearer and as they reached the square hooting and howling, a giant hand reached out of the sky to pluck the riders from the horses' backs.

"I have been in the dark. Alone. No angels met me. No voice answered my calls. *Elohim!*" the rebbe screamed. "*Elohim!* Master of the Universe."

"Oh, Israel," Sarah said. "The Lord tests the righteous. Rabbi Jonathan said the potter does not test cracked pots, because if he tapped it even once it would break. But he does test the good ones because no matter how many times he tests them they do not break. So God tests not the wicked but the righteous."

"You are saying that Rabbi Jonathan thinks I am like a clay pot?"

"Turn on the light," Sarah said, exasperated. "Yitzchak has been waiting to see you."

"In my distress I cried unto the Lord and he did *not* hear me," the rebbe said, misquoting the first line of Psalm 120.

Yitzchak was the rebbe's nephew and only heir to the leadership of the Dokszycer dynasty since the rebbe's son had left the closed walls of the community for the greener shores of New York's Long Island. The rebbe wore his shirt torn in the corner every day as if his only son had died.

Yitzchak was whip thin and as tall as Solomon the Wise was said to have been, though not nearly as sharp, the rebbe often observed. He entered the rebbe's room with an unusual spring in his step.

"How are you feeling today?" he asked. His suit was rumpled and the rebbe could see a soup stain on the front of his shirt.

The rebbe pulled himself up, so that he sat leaning against a couple of pillows. "How am I feeling?" he asked. "Has the Messiah arrived yet?"

"How is your back? And neck?"

The rebbe threw out his arm in a weak backhand and released from his lips a long agonized "Aaaaaaaach!"

"I have found someone," Yitzchak said, smiling and then covering his mouth with his hand. His teeth were as large as those of a horse and the rebbe often joked that he should pray with his mouth closed so he would not scare God from the world. "I have found someone who can help you, Rebbe."

"Only God can help me," the rebbe said, shaking his head slowly until he had to stop from the pain.

"I have found someone," Yitzchak repeated.

"I'm sure you have found someone," the rebbe said.

"I met him at Zion Square," Yitzchak said. "Demonstrating tricks concerning the back."

"No more tricks," the rebbe said.

"He is a healer," Yitzchak said, picking up the edge of the rebbe's bedside table with one shaking hand, spilling a half-full glass of water onto the floor. "Last week, I could not have lifted this."

An hour later Sarah entered, drew the curtains, turned on a small lamp, and led a tall pale man dressed all in white into the rebbe's room.

The rebbe sat propped against his pillows, wearing only his bedclothes and a black *kippah* on his head. He had never seen a grown man so clean shaven. He thought the man looked like a glass of milk. His hair was blond and cropped short and he wore round steel-rimmed spectacles tightly on his face.

"Hello," the man said. "I have come to help you. Doctor John J. McGraw. "

The rebbe had passed the war years as a child in England and spoke English fairly well.

"You have come to help me?" the rebbe said.

"Have you been in bed since you hurt your back?" Dr. John J. McGraw asked. The rebbe nodded. "Sit up on the edge of the bed."

"Why?" the rebbe said.

"Don't be an old goat," Sarah said. "He is trying to help you."

"I can't. I am broken," the rebbe said.

"Very slowly," the doctor said slowly. "You must get out of bed. There is nothing worse for a sore back than immobility."

"Nu?" Sarah said, leaning close to her husband.

"Wife. Leave us," the rebbe said, and then he slid to the edge of the bed.

"Remove your shirt and stand up," the doctor said with such authority that the rebbe didn't question, and stepped into a pair of slippers before pulling off his shirt. Nobody had spoken to him that way since he was a child. He felt small and naked and immediately wanted to cover himself. The doctor told him to drop his hands to his sides.

"Close your eyes," the doctor said.

"My eyes?" the rebbe said. "I'm sure it is not my eyes."

"Close your eyes," the doctor said, and reached under the rebbe's beard, placing his fingers beneath his chin to lift it straight. "Turn your head to the left."

"But it is hurting," the rebbe said.

"Turn your head to the left, and then to the right."

He could feel his nose grazing the doctor's hand on either side as he turned.

"Now, look straight ahead and open your eyes," the doctor said, flatly.

The rebbe was shocked to see that when he opened his eyes, he was not looking straight ahead but down and to the right, toward a pile of dirty laundry.

"I can help you," the doctor said, removing a small silver camera from his pocket.

"What are you doing?" the rebbe said.

"I am going to take a picture of your posture as it is now," the doctor said, aiming the camera. "Look at the curve in your back, and the way your shoulders —"

"No. No!" the rebbe said. "You can't do that. It is against the Second Commandment."

"Just to record your progress," the doctor said.

"No graven images," the rebbe said, turning away.

The doctor put his camera away and apologized to the rebbe. "I am sorry. I am very sorry."

The rebbe looked into the doctor's eyes for the first time, and they were blue and shining like the springtime pools of his youth. He wore some sort of silver charm around his neck that was shaped like the English letter "t." The rebbe shuddered and again thought back to his youth.

"McGraw," the rebbe said, pronouncing the name for the first time. "Where do you come from?"

"Saint Louis."

"I believe there really are Jews everywhere," the rebbe said, smiling.

"I'm not Jewish," the doctor said. "You can put your shirt on now."

"Well, why are you here?" the rebbe said, not quite understanding. He noticed that the doctor's breath smelled like peppermint. "Why did you come to me?"

"I practice the art of correcting," the doctor said. "I

locate spinal malfunction and fix it. Do you have frequent back and neck pain? Do you have pain in between your shoulder blades? Do you feel a numbing or tingling in the arms or hands?"

"Yes! Yes! Yes!" the rebbe screamed.

"Israel, are you all right?" Sarah called from outside the door.

"I am fine, wife." The rebbe pulled his shirt over his head, forgetting his beard inside his nightshirt. "How are you going to help me?"

The doctor explained how nerves connecting to the spine, when pinched or compressed, can cause pain or irritation in almost any part of the body, and how he simply, through controlled pressure, restores the spine to a more normal position, in turn reducing pain and irritation.

"Imagine a garden hose as a nerve and the water flowing through it as the nerve impulses —"

"A what?" the rebbe said.

"A garden hose," the doctor said.

"Do you see a garden around here?" the rebbe said. "In Jerusalem, everything is stone."

"But you are made of flesh and bone," the doctor said. "We must ease the pressure on the nerve. This will take some time. Maybe a week, maybe a few months. Your spine is curving like a question mark."

"A question mark, huh? I have a question for you," the rebbe said, reaching out toward the doctor. "Do you mean you can fix my back?"

"You must have faith."

The doctor walked around behind the rebbe, told him to place his arms across his chest in the form of an "x." He pressed himself close to him and reached around the rebbe. Placing one pale hand on top of the rebbe's and one between his shoulder blades, he pulled in and thrust forward at the exact same moment. There was a pop, pop, and the rebbe screamed out.

"That feels good," the rebbe said, after a moment.

"You should come to my office," the doctor said. "For a complete adjustment, to prevent it from being hurt again."

"But I feel fine," the rebbe said, kicking up his slippered feet, humming a joyous-sounding *nigun* under his breath. "The just among Gentiles are priests of God. Thank you, thank you," he said, "I am so grateful. How can I pay you?"

"You will find a way," the doctor said, removing his glasses to clean them with a handkerchief.

"But a physician who takes no fee is worth no fee."

"I am no physician," the doctor replied.

But the rebbe was so happy, he sang, "I feel so good, I feel so good," and called out for Sarah. "Wife, come look! I feel strong as an ox! Thank you, thank you," he said again to the doctor, who just stood silently, looking about the room.

"You have some very curious objects here," the doctor said, motioning to the rebbe's Galician spice box on the dressing table.

Sarah rushed in, still holding a wooden spoon in her hand. "Israel, I've never seen you so happy," she cried.

"I have found my youth again."

The doctor shook the rebbe's hand, and before walking out of the room, tapped him lightly on the back with his index finger. "Until next time," he said.

Within a few hours, not long after the sirens began wailing throughout the city to announce the sabbath, the rebbe was on his back again, moaning in pain. He had tried to pull himself into his Shabbat finery but fell back onto his bed, where he lay all of Saturday and Sunday. The clanging church bells of the Holy Sepulcher were like mosquitoes in his ears that day in bed, as he lay in the dark with one pillow arching his neck and another covering his face.

Several acres of the Jerusalem forest had caught fire in the dry heat, and the smell of smoke woke the rebbe early Monday morning. Dr. John J. McGraw knocked on the rebbe's door soon afterward. At first, Sarah would not let him pass, and raised her voice when he offered to adjust her and fix her dowager's hump. But finally she relented when the rebbe called, "Let him come."

The stubborn rebbe had piled two pillows onto a chair and sat on them, where he hunched over a small table covered with an open copy of the Talmud. The rebbe looked up and squinted at the doctor. The doctor was dressed in a white shirt with beige pants and looked like nobody the rebbe had ever known. He was thin and plain-looking, like a slice of his wife's challah waiting to be buttered.

"You?" the rebbe said. "I waited for you yesterday. But I couldn't wait," he said, pointing to the pillows beneath him.

"How do you feel?" the doctor said, stepping forward. And for a moment his glasses caught the overhead light and a glare flashed into the rebbe's eyes.

"I feel like I'm sitting on a cloud," the rebbe said. "Filled with fire."

The doctor stepped closer, reached into the rebbe's beard, and placed two fingers beneath the rebbe's chin, raising it. "Do you read like that all the time?"

"Yes, yes," the rebbe said. "I am in very close study."

"Stand up," the doctor said. "You should never read like that."

He led the rebbe to the center of the room. "Does it hurt to walk?"

"Only when I walk."

He placed the rebbe's arms across his chest as he had the first time, and pressed himself close enough that the rebbe noticed that the minty smell had been replaced by cinnamon. The doctor pulled in and thrust forward, and again there was a pop, pop. But this time, the rebbe did not scream out. He simply said, "*Baruch Hashem,* Praise God."

"And now we must walk."

Out in the streets of the shabbiest section of the Mea Shearim quarter, the rebbe walked beside Dr. John J. McGraw. He shuffled his feet at first and then took baby steps, before his feet stuck to the ground not a block from where he lived. A pink stretchy substance clung to the bottom of the rebbe's shoe. "That's mine," the doctor said apologetically, pulling the gum off the rebbe's shoe with a handkerchief. "I spit it out on my way over."

Before long, the rebbe strode like a young man at the side of the doctor. They passed gray stone walls plastered with Yiddish-language posters, walked beneath caged-in balconies where children cried from above, stepped over potholes in the road. They passed bearded men in striped caftans, a woman with a scarf on her head carrying grocery bags, a couple of young yeshiva students bent almost double from the weight of their books, and then a red-bearded Bratzlaver whom the rebbe knew from prayers at the Wall.

"They all do not see me," the rebbe said. "You would think the sun had gone out."

They walked as far as the Street of Prophets, and then turned around, walking back toward the sky blackened with smoke. When they reached a small synagogue not far from the rebbe's home, where the sound of prayers floated out the open windows and into the street, the rebbe stopped to catch his breath.

"My back feels okay. But my lungs, they're bursting."

The doctor peered into the window and began to laugh. "Like pecking chickens," he said under his breath. The rebbe joined him at the window. He had prayed there many times before and saw men bobbing and swaying as if their prayers were taking them very far away. Others sat hunched over large leather-bound books searching for hidden wisdom. The rebbe felt a pain in his heart.

"The Torah says, 'If you forsake me for a single day, I will forsake you for two days,'" the rebbe said. "It has now been six days."

The doctor wiped his brow with a handkerchief. "Look at them," he said, arching his neck to get a better view. Praying men moved like rusty engines and lifted piles of books as if they would collapse under their weight. The doctor turned to the rebbe. "They only need one book. I imagine they feel as much pain as you."

"But I feel pain *not* praying," the rebbe said.

"I will help you fix that," the doctor said, touching him lightly on the back. "But you mustn't shrug your shoulders like that."

The next morning when Dr. John J. McGraw arrived to treat the Dokszycer rebbe, Sarah told him to wait.

"The rebbe is not feeling well," she said. "His back is sore again."

Overhearing his wife in the hallway, the rebbe called, "Let him come."

The rebbe stood gingerly beside his bed wrapping the leather straps of his tefillin around his left arm.

"I don't mean to interrupt," the doctor said, as he entered the rebbe's room. "But what are you doing?"

The rebbe placed the second box of the tefillin onto his forehead and said, "I am putting on my tefillin. And then I am going to pray."

"How is your back today?"

"It hurts," the rebbe said, tightening the straps.

The doctor stepped forward and touched the rebbe's arm where the leather straps were wound tightly against his skin. He walked around behind the rebbe and tapped him between the shoulder blades. "Can you touch your toes?"

"I am trying to pray."

"I can see the tension in your shoulders," the doctor said. "Prayer should not mean pain."

The rebbe smelled cinnamon and felt a sickness in his stomach. "Don't you know there is pain in everything?"

"There doesn't have to be. Those straps are too tight. Look how your body is being pulled to the left, while you lean to the right. The vein in your neck is like a rope," the doctor said, starting to unwind the straps from the rebbe's arm. His nose was so small it looked like it belonged to a young child. "And when you bend over you must remember to bend your knees."

"Bend my knees?"

"Become flexible, and then pray. Like supple reeds on the banks of the Jordan."

He had finished unwrapping the straps of the tefillin

from the rebbe's head and laid the two boxes on the cluttered table beside them.

"But I must say the blessing," the rebbe said. "It is a mitzvah."

Dr. John J. McGraw hesitated and said, "Finish quickly then."

After the rebbe completed his prayers the doctor adjusted him, making tiny pops in his back and neck.

"Good," the doctor said. "When you are ready I will bring you to my office for a thorough adjustment."

"What will happen then?" the rebbe asked.

"Prayer," the doctor said. "Painless prayer."

The doctor showed the rebbe how to stretch his back simply by lying face down on the floor and pushing up with his hands. The rebbe hesitated at first, saying he felt like an animal, but relented when he felt the warm stretch in the muscles of his back. He learned to stretch his calves, neck, and pectorals, and wondered how he could not have known to do something so simple.

Afterward they walked under a hot June sun, through the cluttered streets of Mea Shearim, past the Street of Prophets as far as the British Council Library and the Ethiopian church.

The next morning, the rebbe rose early, wound himself in the leather straps of his tefillin, and muttered the prayers under his breath. As he lay on the floor stretching his back the rebbe wondered if the pinching pain he felt was guilt.

"Good. You've already stretched," the doctor said when he arrived. "We are going to walk a little bit farther today," he added, smiling.

It was already a blazing hot Wednesday morning, as the doctor and the rebbe stepped out of the dingy apartment and into the street. From the doorway Sarah waved a cup and called after the rebbe as he walked away, "Israel, drink some water first! The *hamsiin* has arrived." A dry wind had blown in out of the desert and carried with it a stifling heat that made the asphalt soft beneath their feet. The perfect blue sky was marred intermittently by thin wisps of smoke that rose into the sky like floating Hebrew letters. The sun was already high enough in the sky to bleach all of the stone buildings a harsh, luminous white. There was not a shadow in sight.

The streets of Mea Shearim bustled as usual, as bearded, hat-wearing men dressed in customary black hurried back and forth on their way to or from prayer. Their wives in kerchiefs and long dresses, some pregnant, some not, dragged strollers piled high with children and bags from the market.

The rebbe smiled at a pair of passing men whose noses were buried in prayer books. "Isn't it wonderful," the rebbe said. "Jews everywhere."

"It is wonderful," the doctor said, suddenly beaming.

"Tell me," the rebbe said. "How does a Gentile find himself living in Jerusalem."

"I came to be here for the millennium."

"The millennium?" the rebbe said, confused.

"The year two thousand," the doctor said, ushering the rebbe out of one of the neighborhood's many gates.

"Oh-ho," the rebbe said, laughing. "Two thousand years since . . . It is funny, it must be ten years since I have seen your calendar. For us, for Jews, it is the year fifty-seven sixty."

"And your Messiah has still not arrived."

"Today," the rebbe said. "I am absolutely sure he will arrive today. I have been absolutely sure of that every day for the last sixty-three years. If not today, then tomorrow, which when it arrives," the rebbe said in a singsong manner, "will be today."

"Tell me, what will happen when your Messiah comes?"

"Of course, the Temple will be rebuilt. And we will have a King of Israel at last, and the entire world will be full of the knowledge of the Lord," the rebbe said nonchalantly. "And yours?"

"Exactly the same," the doctor said. "It is written that the Lord Jesus Christ will return to a hill east of Jerusalem and redeem the world."

"And how will you know it is him?" the rebbe said.

"I will look at his hands and at his side, and see if the scars are there. And if there are scars —"

"Enough," the rebbe said, laughing. "Enough of this. Let's turn around. I'm tired of walking today."

They stopped just short of the walls of the Old City, near Damascus Gate, where the doctor offered him a sip of his water. The rebbe was sweating in streams, and gulped down most of the bottle. The sun was still directly above their heads, and felt to the rebbe as if a thousand-pound weight were on his shoulders. They began slowly walking back up the sloping hill.

"Do you know there is a way to walk all around Jerusalem without walking up a hill?" the rebbe said.

"And have you found that way?"

"No."

"Take off your coat and hat. It is too hot for you to wear wool on a day like this."

"But I always wear this," the rebbe said, refusing to remove his heavy wool coat. "I have worn it for hundreds of years."

The next morning, Sarah waited until the rebbe had finished his prayers.

"Israel," she said. "Nobody has seen Yitzchak for days. Do you know where he is?"

The rebbe was in a foul mood as he unwound the tefillin from his aching arm. Aside from his back still aching, now the muscles of his legs were sore. "What, am I Yitzchak's keeper? Do I know where he is every minute of the day? He is a young man, so he is out praying. Maybe he went to Shchem, maybe he went to Hevron. His cousin is living there."

"But nobody has seen him," Sarah said. "Nobody knows where he is. We must find him. Last week a yeshiva boy from Sanhedria was found stabbed in the street."

"All right, all right, wife, I will call Schmuelik, I will call Reuven, I'll call everybody. We will turn the world over, if that's what you want."

And that was when the doctor walked in, looking red and childlike, burned from the sun. The rebbe wanted to say, "Now you know why we wear the coats?"

"Your door was open," the doctor said. "Are you ready to go?"

"I'm not going anywhere today. Now besides my back hurting and my neck hurting and my arms hurting, my legs are hurting, and precious Yitzchak is missing and we must find him, because if we don't find him, my wife will never let me sleep."

"You shouldn't wave your arms like that," the doctor said, with his arms still at his sides. "It will throw your whole body out of alignment. We must continue to strengthen your back. You are doing so well. In a few more days, your back will be as strong as a tree, and the adjustments will hold."

"Ach, the forest is burning," the rebbe said. "Today my business is Yitzchak. Surely you can wait until tomorrow to make me better. If you want, you can make the popping in my back."

"It's important that we continue to build your strength. We have come so far."

The rebbe asked Sarah to leave the room, turned his back to the doctor, and crossed his arms over his chest.

"The rebbe is asking you to pop him quickly," the rebbe sang, "and tomorrow you will return to walk with him. But right now, he must find Yitzchak."

The doctor pressed himself close to the rebbe, took his crossed arms in his hands and thrust in with supernatural force. The rebbe screamed out in pain, and felt like he was being broken to pieces. He actually called out for his mother, and then fell to the floor. "What have you done to me?"

"Tomorrow, we will walk," the doctor said, and lifted the rebbe up. He placed a hot hand between his shoulder blades, pushed in slightly, and left the stunned rebbe alone in his room.

The Dokszycers searched synagogues and study halls from Pisgat Ze'ev to Efrat but did not find Yitzchak nor any sign of him that day. But the rebbe said not to worry, there are not many places Yitzchak could go.

Friday morning the doctor arrived as promised. The rebbe had not slept at all the night before. He had tossed and turned in his bed thinking of Yitzchak and the doctor and Sarah, who had yelled at him while he stretched on the floor, telling him to get up, he looked like a snake. She was angry that he would not spend another day searching for Yitzchak, who would have to spend Shabbat among strangers.

The rebbe appeared wearing a plain white shirt, buttoned to the top, and a pair of black suspenders. On his head he wore only a large black silken *kippah* pulled low over his brow covering his hairline. His heavy wool coat and large-brimmed black hat lay on top of the rebbe's bed like a sick or dying man.

"We are walking farther today?" the rebbe asked.

"If you are ready," the doctor said.

"Look," the rebbe said, pointing to a bottle hooked to his belt. "Water."

The doctor adjusted the rebbe's back, repeating, "Good, good," as he worked.

"Hurry back," Sarah called after the doctor and the rebbe, but they didn't hear, lost as they were in discussion.

"So you are saying that Jesus was the son of God and is the Messiah?" the rebbe said rhetorically as he mopped his forehead with a handkerchief.

The doctor nodded his head.

"So the Messiah has come?" the rebbe said.

"Yes."

They walked in silence for a few moments through the buzzing quarter of Mea Shearim, where men hurried off to pray before the sabbath and the women frantically rushed about buying food for their Shabbat tables.

"No," the rebbe said. "The Messiah has not come. Because if He had, the world would be a very different place. So your Messiah has not come. So you wait."

They arrived a while later at Damascus Gate. Even the cool-blooded doctor was sweating now, as they stepped down toward the massive entrance to the Old City. Young Arab men joked and pulled their kaffiyehs around their faces against the gray smoke that still swam through the city. Women sat on the ground along the entryway, selling fruits and vegetables on outspread headscarves. An Israeli soldier sat languidly in an opening above the entrance and picked his teeth with a telephone card. They entered the ornamented stone gate and were immediately swallowed up by pressing crowds and the tinny sounds of Arabic music. The air smelled to the rebbe like barbecued meat. It was the Muslim sabbath and thousands of men dressed in kaffiyehs inched their way toward the Dome of the Rock to pray to the mighty Allah. This was the way the rebbe always walked to the Western Wall, but had never been that way on a Friday morning. Bearded kaffiyeh-wearing men pressed forward, their ragged caftans flapping as they walked. An old man waved his arms, shouting loudly in Arabic. The rebbe looked over at the doctor and saw his milk-dish of a face contorted with fear. The rebbe, too, felt unease in the pit of his belly and reached out to take the doctor's hand in his, so as not to lose him.

They turned into a small street and the rebbe let go of the doctor's hand. Immediately the crowds and the smells of spice and Turkish coffee were gone. The street narrowed and then widened out again. A group of men and women dressed in white and beige, topped with gaudy sunhats, moved toward the rebbe and the smiling doctor. They were singing hymns and several dragged a large wooden cross. "That can't be good for the back," the rebbe thought, stopping to catch his breath. He stared around in wonder. These people, pale and plain as cotton balls, nodded their heads to the doctor as they passed. Who were they? One man wearing round glasses like the doctor pulled out a camera and shot a quick picture of the rebbe standing beside the Third Station of the Cross.

"What?" the rebbe screamed. "What are you doing?"

The man smiled and took another picture. The rebbe screamed again, a curse so ancient that even he did not know its meaning, and then he charged at the man, kicked at him, and jumped on his back. The doctor pulled the rebbe away, almost throwing him onto the ground as the group scattered.

"My back," the rebbe said, from the ground where he lay awkwardly on his side. "Ohhhhh! My broken back."

"Like the agony of Christ," the doctor said, smiling. "This is where Jesus fell for the first time."

"My back, my back! What are you, crazy? Take me home."

"Do you want to be saved?"

"Yes. Pop my back. Please pop it."

"God made his original covenant with a Jew," the doctor said. "And now it is time to renew that covenant."

"Pop my back!" the rebbe screamed. "Pop it. I must go home."

"Do you know that even from here on the Via Dolorosa, you can hear the Shabbat sirens sounding for the Jewish sabbath. I can leave you here," the doctor said. "Or, I can pop your back now and you will come to my office for a final adjustment. It is not far from here."

"What are you going to do?" the rebbe said, wincing in pain.

"I will fix you so you do not feel pain when you pray," the doctor said.

The rebbe paused for a moment and looked down at the stones beneath him. He stood up. "Okay. I will go. But I must be home by Shabbat. Now, please pop my back. I am broken in two."

The doctor moved in behind the rebbe and placed his hand between his shoulder blades and thrust forward as he pulled in from the front. "Now we will walk."

"Who were those people? Who was the man with the camera?" the rebbe asked, and took a long drink of his water.

"Pilgrims," the doctor answered. "Holy pilgrims."

As they passed the Condemnation Chapel and the Chapel of the Flagellation, the doctor excitedly explained the importance of the buildings. "And just over there is Our Lady of the Spasm."

"Spasm?" the rebbe thought. "What is this, sick? Flagellation, condemnation?"

Then they passed the Church of Saint Anne and left the walled city through Saint Stephen's Gate.

"There is the Garden of Gethsemane, and the Basilica of the Agony where Jesus was betrayed by a kiss. And of course across the valley, there is the Mount of Olives."

The rebbe knew the Mount of Olives well. He planned to be buried near his father on the western slope facing the Old City. His head began to buzz from thirst and the heat and he wanted to sit down, but he didn't dare, as they were passing through a Muslim cemetery. A shepherd and his flock were fast approaching through the tall, dry grass. "How much farther?"

"Not far. How is your back?" the doctor said, not waiting for an answer as the road sloped down into the valley. "When the Messiah returns, all who are buried here will be resurrected."

"Yes," the rebbe said. "I know that."

They walked in silence down among the cracked Hebrew gravestones. The rebbe read the names to himself and mumbled a silent kaddish for the dead. And though he knew they would one day be returned to the earth he felt a deep sadness for them as there was one thing the dead could not do. They could not perform God's mitzvah of prayer.

After noticing a grave marked with the name Ben David, the rebbe bent over and placed a stone on the grave. "Our Messiah must come from the house of David."

"The same as Jesus," the doctor said.

The rebbe turned around and faced the Old City. The sun was finally starting to move down the sky toward the west and he removed his *kippah* for a moment and mopped the sweat from his brow. "There. You see." He pointed vaguely toward the city. "The sealed gate. It is called the Gate of Mercy. That is the gate the Messiah will use when he at last enters Jerusalem."

"The same gate that Jesus last used when he entered Jerusalem," the doctor answered. "You see. We are just splitting hairs."

They walked farther up the mount, the rebbe close on the heels of the doctor as he drank the last of his water. The rebbe's beard felt as heavy as stone against his chest. When they crested the hill they could easily see the black smoke rising from the forest to the west as the fires moved slowly toward Tel Aviv.

"Blessed are the humble-minded, for they will possess the land," the doctor said, his voice rising. "Blessed are those who are hungry and thirsty for uprightness, for they will be satisfied. Blessed are the merciful, for they will be shown mercy. Blessed are the pure of heart, for they will see God."

"That is beautiful," the rebbe said.

The doctor smiled. "You have reached the top. Look!"

The rebbe looked out beyond the Valley of Kidron and saw the Old City and the shining gold of the Dome of the Rock and imagined a time before the walls and the city when Abraham, a simple man, answered a call from the wilderness and was tested.

The doctor put his arm around the rebbe and said, "We are very much alike." They began walking toward a white arched building at the end of a gravel road. "Prayer is the backbone of your life, and prayer is the heart of my life. Look to the west. It is burning. They are sinning in Tel Aviv, they are sinning in London, they are sinning in New York. But here in Jerusalem, in this prayer factory, there is goodness. It is us against them. Those who will live and those who will die."

They arrived outside of the new hastily constructed Resurrection Hotel that had been built to accommodate the thousands of expected pilgrims arriving to celebrate the millennium and await the Resurrection.

"You know, there is only one God," the doctor said. "It is just that you are praying in the wrong language, so to speak, in an awkward manner. Look at how these prayers have twisted your body. I know that terrible things have happened to the Jews. Terrible tragedies. Because your prayers simply went poof, into the sky. Nobody was listening."

"Many strayed from the path," the rebbe said, sadly. "But I am a good person. I perform all six hundred thirteen of God's commandments."

"But it is time for a new covenant," the doctor said, leading the rebbe under the archway into the Resurrection Hotel.

The hotel lobby was sparsely decorated and shabby. It looked as if the furniture had been borrowed from another hotel. Several plain-looking people dressed in drab colors and comfortable shoes lingered in the lobby, talking quietly.

"*Vus nu?*" the rebbe said, raising his voice to break the silence of the cool lobby. "What now?"

"My office is just down this corridor," the doctor said, leading the rebbe to a wooden door where a sign hung that said: HOLY MISSION CHIROPRACTIC.

The doctor opened the door and the rebbe followed, feeling faint. There was another closed door across the room, emblazoned with a golden crucifix. The rebbe stood stunned. He felt that he was in another land, far from home.

"Would you like some water?" the doctor said, pulling a paper cone from beside the water cooler.

"No, no," the rebbe said. "I will be okay."

"I know you will. I must apologize," the doctor said, gesturing toward the closed door. "It seems my colleague is in with a patient. He will not be long."

The rebbe began to sway back and forth and mumble under his breath as he moved. He felt a pain in his spine, but it was a good pain, a familiar pain, a pain that belonged to him.

The doctor smiled and said, "You are praying again," and dropped a cushion on the floor before them. "Let me show you how."

The doctor fell to his knees on the cushion and placed the palms of his hands together. He looked up at the rebbe. "It is easy. And it does not hurt."

"No," the rebbe said. "No!"

"It says in Revelations that the conversion of the Jews will herald the coming of Christ," the doctor said. "Please kneel."

The door opened, and out stepped the man who had photographed the rebbe on the Via Dolorosa. Behind him, in the center of the room, the rebbe could see tilted to an almost vertical position on the chiropractic table, Yitzchak, precious Yitzchak, smiling a horse-toothed smile, with his arms outstretched to meet the rebbe.

"He has been adjusted," the man said. "Is your patient ready, Doctor McGraw?"

"Yitzchak!" the rebbe called, and sang out the Shema, "Hear, O Israel: the Lord our God. The Lord is One," as loud as he could both forward and backward, as he had been told his great-great-grandfather, may his memory blessed, had done to vanquish the cossacks in the town square of Dok-szyce all those years ago.

The Ascent
of Eli Israel

Toward Jerusalem

SPRING WAS IN FULL FLAME AGAIN and Eli was a shepherd at Betar, south of Jerusalem, but up even higher in the sky. His friend Zev knew a man who had a flock of sheep out over the Green Line, who knew that Eli needed help. He asked if Eli could watch over his sheep. Most of the great leaders in the history of mankind have been shepherds, Eli thought: Abraham, Isaac, Jacob, Moses, David, Joseph. All the twelve tribes, all of Jacob's twelve sons, had been shepherds.

Eli recalled the words of Micah the prophet that said the Lord would come forth from his throne and tread upon the high places of the earth.

So he agreed to go.

"Just melt into the land," Zev had said to Eli. "And you're gone."

Eli fashioned a carpetbag out of an old red, black, and green riding blanket, and tied the heavy load to him with rope. And he herded sheep out there, protecting the Green Line between Israel and the West Bank, with just his wooden staff, an old .38 Special, and his lumpy carpetbag pressing into his back.

It was quiet. He had never heard quiet like this. Every once in a while, some broken-down fellahin would ride by on their donkeys and wave, or an F-15 would buzz the sky overhead, but Eli was alone out there, waiting for his next instruction.

Sometimes a gray wolf would saunter past and sit down. Even in broad daylight. And the wolf wasn't looking at his sheep at all. They would sit and stare at each other for hours, and Eli would ask him questions, questions about life and purity and goodness. He would fall asleep, and when he awoke the wolf would still be there, watching him.

With all the static of the world gone, a simple piece of grass became a thing of monumental beauty. He would hold a single blade in his hand for hours and feel its texture, as smooth as a satin dress then rough as sandpaper, causing his fingers to bleed. He discovered that all the elements of the universe existed inside of everything, and if he looked the right way he could turn a blade of grass into a meal filling enough for a week, or a sky full of stars into an intricate checkerboard that would entertain him until the sky turned blue with morning. He stretched his shadow across the land and ran after it laughing, or ran from it crying. Sometimes, he saw things that he would normally have heard and heard things that he should only have seen.

He could feel God moving throughout creation and would call out, "Do you hear me? Do you hear me?" and tell him how far he had been from him and ask him to bring him closer to his strength.

It had been more than a year since he had been called.

"Eli Haller, son of man. Go to the house of Israel."

He had jumped up off his mother's couch, spilling the scotch he was pouring into a tall glass, and said, "What? Who?"

From the darkness of his aging mother's Brooklyn apartment he heard a heavy silence. His mother's door was still closed, and only the flashing of the muted television lit the room. He lay flat against the floor, his heart beating against the carpet. Over the top of the couch he was able to see that the door was still triple bolted.

"Shit," he said, reaching for the bottle of Dewars on the low glass table beside him. The light and shadows cast upon the ceiling from the streetlights down below seemed to blur and distort before his eyes, like something melting.

The voice came again and he dropped the bottle.

"Who are you?"

The answer was more of a breath than a name. Eli felt it through all of the cells of his body.

"Who are you?" Eli screamed.

The room filled with fire, a black fire radiating darkness, a fire so dark he could only see inside himself, his ribcage heaving, blood racing through the veins, heart pumping, bubbling cells and microcells and the spaces between them. His bones ached, and it was inside him now, a winged pillar of black fire with four faces, looking to the east, west, north, and south. He could see them all at once. One face was a child, the other a man, the third was a lion, and the fourth face an eagle. Four voices joined as one and said, "I am the Lord and I have judged you."

"No," Eli screamed, and tore at his hair, banged his head against the floor. He saw the hurt faces of his wife and child, felt the soft touch of her hand against his cheek. He lifted his face from the carpet, and heard a distant crying that he knew belonged to Josh.

"You have known the dark path," the voice said. "I will

breathe a new spirit into you, remove your heart, and give you a new one. You will walk in my light and follow my laws, and others will, too. And I will be your God and their God."

A wind came and the wings whipped the dark fire into a pillar of burning orange flames. "Those who don't walk my path will know no God and will suffer famine and pestilence and the sword."

When God had gone Eli Haller lay still for hours afterward crying everything into the carpet.

In the City of the Patriarchs

On the bus from the airport, an old rabbi turned his face away from Eli and told him in heavily accented English, "You are dying, friend."

Just after nightfall, the bus dropped Eli off outside a barbed-wire compound at a place called Tel Romeida, which sat on a bluff overlooking downtown Hebron. His body shook beneath a crushing headache as he searched for the home of his only remaining friend in the world. Muezzins began to wail from their minarets under a tangle of faintly blinking stars. Eli forced a stiff-necked nod as he passed bored-looking Israeli soldiers who leaned against gray cement blocks spitting sunflower seed shells into the air.

Eli had managed to find his way to the city of Hebron from the address on an old postcard Zev had sent him in New York.

Zev lived in a caravan on the top of a hill, just above the Arab homes and vineyards clustered together down below. He hugged Eli close to him, saying with a smile, "Brother!

Just in time for the *simcha*." He took the bag from Eli's hand and dropped it to the floor.

"I knew you'd come someday," Zev said, stretching his arms expansively as he whooped: "Welcome to the wild, wild West Bank!"

Zev was still a big man, with giant shoulders and long hair, and could have been Eli's brother or a mirror image only five years older. Now he wore a *kippah* on his head and a long beard with sidecurls at his ears. They had met years back at a John Lennon memorial at Strawberry Fields in Central Park, had prowled the streets of New York, and flunked out of A.A. together. Zev had been at the hospital when Eli's son was born and they'd celebrated together on pills Zev had stolen from the E.R.

Eli covered his ears and said, absently, "You look great, Zev." He felt burning throughout his body, as if his veins were filled with something other than blood. His eyes felt as if they were swathed in cotton.

"I'm doing my best to be my best," Zev said, leading Eli into his home. "You look like shit."

"I do," Eli said, and he wanted to sit down before he fell down. He still heard the voice in his head, but it was in no language he had ever heard.

"What?" Zev said.

"I don't know," Eli said, and was silent for a moment as he looked around at the spartan interior of the caravan. "Is this the house of Israel?"

"This is the house of Zev, man. Come on, take a load off."

"Okay," Eli said, and Zev suddenly looked like some giant biblical Samson. "You look healthy. Really."

"It's the Torah, man," Zev said. "You have no idea." He led Eli to a red plastic chair, and watched him drop into it. "The shiksa?"

"Gone," Eli said.

"The kid?"

"Gone, too."

"Well, he's not Jewish anyway," Zev said, surprising Eli. "Thems the breaks, bubelah."

"What?" Eli said.

"One man's garbage is another man's treasure. I wish her luck," Zev said, ruffling Eli's hair. "Smile, man. You're part of the tribe of the Messiah. We're going to a party. *Sefer Torah,* man. A party for the new Torah scroll. Stick with me. I'll get you back on your feet."

"Let me lie down first."

"You just got here and you're crashing?" Zev said.

"I'm an 'elder statesman of American television,'" Eli said bitterly, quoting the *TV Guide* critic who pronounced his production company, Ellis Hall Home Entertainment, and his Cold War schlock "a dinosaur deader than Ed Sullivan."

"You're only forty-three, dude."

After Eli rested and drank some coffee, he felt somewhat renewed. His footsteps marched in synch with Zev's down the hill past dimly lit Arab homes. They heard children laughing and the sound of televisions blaring in Arabic. Zev pointed out, "This was a Jewish home. This was a Jewish home," as they walked.

The air smelled to Eli like nothing he had ever smelled before, clean and fresh and natural. He felt the cool spring air wash over him and felt healthy for the first time in a long time. He looked up in the sky and the stars seemed closer than they had ever been before.

The synagogue was crammed with black-clad yeshiva *bochers,* and full-bearded men wearing jeans and knitted *kippahs,* like Zev. It was the first time he had been in a synagogue since his bar mitzvah, not long before he left home for good. This was not the way Eli remembered synagogue.

Zev whispered in Eli's ear, "It's like we are actually standing at Sinai waiting for Moshe Rabeynu, our great rabbi of rabbis, Moses to bring us God's commandments. You have no idea how special it is when a Torah scroll is completed. They are not mass produced like some Gideon's Bible, they are written by hand on parchment the same way they have been written since the time of our prophets."

Eli noticed there were no women and thought of his life in New York. His wild days when his shows were doing well: *Spy, Berliner; Hotel Cadillac;* and *Walkabout Willie,* all top ten in the Nielsen ratings. Women constantly. He remembered going on a talk show and admitting he was a sex addict. Later he said he had become a Buddhist. He didn't come home for days at a time, found himself in orgies without even knowing how he got there. His wife was hysterical, threatened to throw him out. It was simple to drink. And then that last night with the prop from the set. Didn't she know he was only playing?

Eli saw a room full of praying men and was thankful that temptation had been removed. Had these men also been called by God? And where was God now, hiding in the parchment of the new Torah scroll? A whining clarinet started up and the men began to dance in spinning circles.

Zev squeezed his hand and pulled him closer to him. "This is great," he shouted. "I can see us together on Judgment Day, riding the lightning with Moshiach."

Eli stood still, trying to maintain his balance. The nap and the coffee had only provided a temporary respite. Zev invited him to join the circle, but he begged off, saying he wanted to watch first. He felt his eyes must have looked like swollen golfballs. His head began to spin again as the men whirled around and around.

"Am Yisrael Chai, Am Yisrael Chai, Am Yisrael, Am Yisrael, Am Yisrael Chai!" they all sang.

Zev pumped his fist from where he stood beside Eli and sang along. The room smelled of sweat and one of the dancers slipped on the floor, flying out of the circle.

"Have some vodka," the man said, gripping a bottle in his hands. Sweat poured down his face from underneath his large-brimmed hat. He looked like a gangster. This can't be what God intended, Eli thought.

"I'm okay," Eli said.

"Drink," he said, climbing to his feet.

"No," Eli said.

"Take a drink," Zev said, taking the bottle in his hands. "Just one."

He gulped at the bottle and a lightning bolt shot straight to his head. He felt adrenaline kick into his heart. The man plunked his hat onto Eli's head and pulled him into the circle. The Torah scroll appeared, carried by a tiny white-bearded man under a blue wedding *huppa,* and the men began to whirl even faster. Eli felt his legs melt beneath him, and then he saw feet blurring all around him.

"Am Yisrael Chai, Am Yisrael Chai, Am Yisrael, Am Yisrael, Am Yisrael Chai!"

Eli survived on olives, almonds, figs, sage, carob, mint leaves, anything he could find in the hilltops and wadis out there in the wilderness. He slept in caves when he could find them, bathed himself in fresh mountain water, and sometimes didn't speak a word aloud for weeks.

One day as he was grazing his sheep on the rough tangled bushes and grasses of the Judean hills, an army jeep pulled to the top of a rocky cliff above him. He could see an Israeli flag standing stiff in the wind. He knew there was no use in running, so he sat among his sheep, staring into the distance. They called and waved him to come up. And now the grass stopped singing to God and Eli's blood began to churn up again.

Zev had warned Eli before he left Hebron not to talk to anyone; Arabs, of course, but especially the army.

"That's my hill," Eli shouted and pointed with his staff to another bare hill. "And that belongs to King David." He had not spoken aloud in such a long time, he was not even sure his voice would carry far enough for them to hear.

He sat on his carpetbag and looked back toward his sheep. The sun was a giant copper disk, pressing down on his head, and he looked toward his .38 lying nearby.

A few minutes later a dark, Sephardi-looking soldier wearing a helmet two sizes too big sauntered down the hill lighting a cigarette. *"Nudnik. Boker tov,"* he called.

Eli called back good morning in English.

The soldier lit another cigarette then took off his helmet

and sat on it near him. He unstrapped his M-16 and laid it on the ground beside him.

Eli's heart began to pump faster than it had since he had come to the wilderness. He could feel his heart squeeze like a fist. He shifted on his pack. Eli thought, this punk is eighteen, nineteen at most. What does he know?

"Nize day. Cigariah?" He held the cigarette out to Eli, who didn't say anything. He noticed that the soldier had a terrible case of acne and a long feminine nose. Two soldiers laughed like camels at the top of the hill and danced to music blasting from Army wave radio.

"You don't smoke," the soldier said with a slow thick accent. "You can't to be here. It's not safe."

"I don't see any Arabs," Eli said. "Just me and my sheep."

"You are paralyzed to an army shooting range," the soldier said.

"You mean 'parallel'?"

"It's not safe," the soldier repeated.

"I'm okay," Eli said. He only wanted the soldiers to go away. But then he thought about his beard, and sidecurls, and the fringes of his *tzitzis* hanging from his pants and realized: these rock 'n' rollers think we all look the same.

"What is that stink?" the soldier said, pinching his nose.

Eli didn't even notice anymore that his bag smelled. He didn't answer.

"Come. Have some tea and nana in the jeep. Let me invite you," the soldier said, pointing up to the jeep.

"No."

"You must not to be here," he said, putting the second cigarette in his mouth. And then one of the other soldiers called to him from the hilltop. "Motti. *Yala! Imshi!*"

He waved him away and said, "You like young girls? Boys? Come to the base. You can't to be here. We have food and beds to sleep."

"What about my sheep?" Eli asked.

"You like fuck sheep?" The soldier laughed. "Okay. Sheep okay."

"Get out of here," Eli said. "My sheep don't eat in a mess hall, and I don't need a bed. The land will take care of us. I can go wherever I want, I'm a Jew on Jewish land."

"It's not safe," the soldier said.

"Safe, not safe. I don't gave a damn."

The soldier looked toward the red, green, and black bag again. Eli shifted uneasily. "That is the Palestine colors," the soldier said, moving closer. "I should take that from you."

"No!" Eli screamed in the upper register.

"I joke," the soldier said, laughing. "Let me help you carry your sack up the hill."

"No," Eli said forcefully.

"Homo," the soldier said, laughing, and ran back to meet his comrades. "You stink."

The jeep drove back toward the road, and Eli could still see them laughing. He picked up his .38 Special from the ground and pointed it toward the soldiers in the jeep as they got smaller and smaller in his sight. "Bang," he whispered. "Bang, bang, bang, bang, bang."

Eli's beard grew in thick and gray and he rested in Zev's bed for the next month. He was restless to answer his God when he first arrived, anxious to walk the land and drink in his wisdom, and he felt God's spirit burning through his veins, but was too weak to move. This must be a joke, Eli thought. I'm here and I can't even get out of bed. He threw up in the mornings and apologized to God: "I'm failing you. I'm sorry." Zev slept on a cot in his makeshift kitchen, cleaned up Eli's vomit, washed his urine-stained sheets, and nursed Eli back to health.

During the first week of his convalescence Eli awoke one night and thought he heard Josh calling, "Daddy!" He rolled over to tell his wife to check on him, but the bed was empty. He could see stars and a glowing moon pasted onto the ceiling, as mysterious as the real night sky, and he remembered he was with Zev in Hebron. It frightened him at first and he rolled over, sure that he smelled Kate on the sheets. He felt emptied out inside and thought out loud, "What do I do now? What do I do now?"

"It's okay, man," Zev called from the kitchen. "Trust in Hashem. God will take care of you."

"Has God ever whispered in your ear?" Eli said, thinking of the voice that sent him to Hebron, the voice that was silent now.

"Every day, brother. Every day," Zev said. "There is nowhere that a Jew can be alone, because wherever he goes, his God is with him."

Eli pulled his pillow close to him, remembering the words, "You will walk in my light and follow my laws, and others will too. And I will be your God and their God."

"Is God with me?" Eli said.

"You betcha."

It began to dawn on him that maybe Zev was one of God's angels, sent to watch over him, to lead him in the right direction.

The next morning Zev began to speak to him of the miracles of Torah study as he fed Eli yogurt and hard-boiled eggs for breakfast.

"The words of the Torah, man, are like golden vessels," Zev said, "and the more you scour them and polish them the more they shine and reflect the face of who looks at them."

Zev brought Eli a new hardcover translation of the Torah, with Hebrew on one side of the page and English on the other. Eli began to read, slowly, bit by bit, of the creation of man, the sacrifice of Abraham, Jacob's blessing of Isaac, the darkness of Egypt, and the Exodus.

He lay propped up against two pillows and thought of his studies as a child for his bar mitzvah. "Are these the same words?" he wondered.

Later, as his mind wandered to the slick bodies of his past, his hand slid down to stroke himself underneath the blanket.

"You're gonna want to save that."

Eli stopped.

The voice?

It was only Zev standing in the doorway. "You're not going to flush a nation down the toilet."

Zev lit candles for Shabbat and taught Eli the prayer inviting the sabbath bride.

Eli's fever began to break near the end of Shabbat and Zev brought in a spice box for him to smell.

"How are you feeling?" Zev asked, taking a sniff from the silver spice box.

"Better," Eli answered. "But awful."

"You're back in the world, man," Zev said, smiling. "Your eyes are starting to shine again. You know, Torah can do all sorts of miracles, fighting sickness and degradation, even the Angel of Death. Saved my life."

The last time Eli had seen Zev before he came to Hebron, Zev was drinking heavily and eating from restaurant Dumpsters. He was in and out of jail. Then one night, under the glow of a big autumn moon, he said, "Going to see the rebbe," and wandered off.

"Something inside me just told me it was time," Zev said. "I went to Brooklyn, man. Met the Lubavitcher rebbe and started studying Torah."

Eli learned that Hebron was the first Jewish city and that Abraham bought a field and a cave near Tel Romeida from Ephron the Hittite, and that later his wife and descendants down to Jacob were buried on that land. He learned there was a massacre in 1929 where Jews were torn to pieces by their Arab neighbors after living side by side with them for hundreds of years, and that the Israeli government did not want Jews to resettle and live in Hebron, the City of the Patriarchs.

If Jews were told that they couldn't live in one of the five boroughs of New York, Eli thought, if they were told that it was being reserved for blacks and Puerto Ricans and Jews couldn't live there, people would call it anti-Semitism, racism. So, why shouldn't I live here, he thought?

When Eli was well enough, Zev took him to the *mikvah* and he immersed himself in the cleansing waters of the bath, feeling a new energy flowing through his body. He passed his days studying the words of the Lord and his prophets and began to realize the profound mistakes he had made in his past life. In the book of Hosea he learned that since he had forgotten God and married a Gentile, God would forget his child. He learned in Isaiah that he had been arrogant in his wealth, supplanting God with material gains, and that for punishment he would be "brought down to the nether-world, to the uttermost parts of the pit." Eli remembered the darkest days after his wife threw him out and he thanked God for bringing him close to his breast. He sang psalms of praise with Zev and slept with the words of the Lord burned into his brain.

He wore his beard long and a *kippah* on his head, and prayed daily at the Tomb of Machpelah, the burial place for Abraham, Isaac, Jacob, and their wives. When he wasn't pray-ing he walked the streets of Hebron. One day a man spat in his face, called him a "Zionist pig," and cursed at him in Ara-bic. Eli ran after him, but lost the man in a crowd. He felt proud to be wearing a *kippah*. He wandered into the Casbah and the merchants would not sell him their wares. He saw a camel hanging upside down from a hook with its intestines spilling from its sides like extension cords and felt nauseated. Children laughed like monkeys and shouted at him as he passed. Eli wondered what God had in mind when he made the Arabs.

Zev and Eli went for lunch with a rabbi and his wife who lived over at Shilo. The rabbi had planted a bomb that had blown the legs off of an Arab mayor in the eighties and had served thirty months in prison.

Eli could not imagine spending thirty minutes in prison. The walls would close in on him and he would be alone inside his head. Eli would never go to prison. Never.

"I don't want to be a fascist, but I have no choice," the

rabbi had said. "God gave this land to Abraham and the Jewish people, forever."

"Forever," Zev added, popping an olive in his mouth.

"Listen," the rabbi said, turning to Eli, "as long as we have this secular system, we are going to have chaos. The waters of Babylon are rising."

"This is the Holy Land, man," Zev said. "Put it back in God's hands and give him the respect. If you want to be secular, go to America."

"I'm done with that," Eli said. "Sodom and Gomorrah."

"You said it, brother," Zev said. "Hey, today's leaders, they haven't even gone to any kind of leadership school. They're just buying their way into politics and government."

"Amen," Eli said.

"Amen," the rabbi said, standing up from the table.

About a month before the prime minister was assassinated Eli and Zev went to a rally in Jerusalem where thousands of people crowded forward, fists raised in the air, as a man shouted from a podium before a placard that said: **DANGER! ALL HANDS TO THE DEFENSE OF JERUSALEM!** Their voices all raised as one, cheering at intervals. Their cries rising and falling like waves. Eli smelled something burning and saw gray smoke snaking into the sky.

"They're saying the prime minister is the son of an Arab and a Nazi," Zev said to Eli, a cigarette burning between his lips. "You can't trade land that God gave Abraham for a piece of paper."

The smoke carried a terrible odor over the crowd and smelled like something rotten and foul.

The crowd let up a roar and Eli felt waves rolling throughout his body. They were burning the prime minister in effigy and the crowd rushed forward, smashing at the body with sticks until it was beaten to the ground.

Eli had never felt this connected to anything in his life before, even when the Yankees won the World Series in 1977. He raised his fist in the air and shouted out, "Rabin the traitor, Rabin the traitor."

During the curfew, Eli and Zev walked alone through the streets, sloping down to the Beit Hadassah compound where other Jews lived. Zev's Uzi submachine gun bounced against his back as he walked.

"Enjoy this," Zev said, "this quiet won't last. If you listen carefully, you can hear the violence sizzling in the air."

He felt proud, walking through the streets with Zev. This was not the Judaism he remembered.

Eli thought of the schoolyard in eighth grade when Connor Peters hit him in the head with a roll of pennies and pushed him to the ground shouting, "Pick 'em up, Jew," as a group of fifth and sixth graders laughed at him. *Is this what a Jew is?* Eli had thought. He picked up a stone, pulled himself off the ground, and slammed the stone into Connor's face. Eli remembered that the laughing stopped.

When his father came to get him from the principal's office, he saw the two boys; Connor holding a bloody rag to his face, and Eli sitting quietly on the bench. His father looked at Eli with his frozen blue eyes, crossed his arms to cover his tattoo, and said in his thick accent, "Apolochize."

At that moment, Eli hated his father. He felt his father had failed a mighty test and had revealed the true nature of the mystery of what it meant to be a Jew.

On al-Shuhada Street, "the street of the martyrs," Eli and Zev passed shuttered storefronts spray-painted with Stars of David, some had fists painted inside them. A donkey poked his head out over a low wire fence and brayed. They passed more graffiti in red: "RABIN IS AN ARAB!" "KAHANE LIVES!" "DEPORT, KILL ARABS!" and then sloppily written and partially crossed out, "WITH BLOOD AND FIRE, JEWS OUT."

To their right, beyond a run-down cemetery, tiny lights flickered inside the bare-faced concrete pillboxes of Arab homes stacked up into the Hebron hills. The March air was cool and damp and Eli pulled his parka closed. He wondered if the inside of their homes looked as much like prisons as the outside.

They walked into the depths of the Arab casbah, their footsteps echoing on the empty streets. Vegetables rotted on their wagons and the air smelled foul. Eli leaped behind one of the wooden carts and began to bark out prices like one of the Arab merchants. "Special price," he laughed. "Special price for Jew," and he spat into a pile of rotting tomatoes.

Zev didn't laugh but kept on walking and lit a cigarette. A puff of smoke rose above his head. "Over fifty people killed on their way to work. Real holy," he said.

The curfew had been in place for more than a week now, since the two buses had been blown up in Jerusalem. A muezzin began to wail *"Ull-aaaaaaw-hoo-Ak-bar! Ull-aaaaaaw-hoo-Ak-bar!"*

It seemed that the volume on the minaret speakers had been turned up again.

"These kids are being brainwashed," Zev shouted. "Do you know what kind of gutter religion we are talking about? Do you know what they are being told? That their reward for killing Jews will be seventy-two virgins waiting for them in heaven."

"I didn't know there were any virgins left," Eli said, and they both laughed.

He thought of Josh back on Long Island and the time he had set fire to a pile of old newspapers in the garage. Eli had grounded him and taken away his allowance for a month, but he was on the streets playing again in a week.

"Listen up, and listen good, brother," Zev said. "Nobody ever screwed in heaven. It's all lies. Bubbe meysehs!"

Eli was far away now, even as they reached an army checkpoint and the high walls of the Tomb of Machpelah. Josh would be thirteen this week, and Eli didn't even know where he was.

"You've got to take away their keys to heaven," Zev continued, "you've got to get them while they're still in bed, or while they're preparing for their deaths."

He should have his bar mitzvah soon, Eli thought.

"You should bury the bombers inside pig skins," Zev continued. "Then they'll think twice about the glories of heaven."

Eli was silent for a moment and then said, "This doesn't sound like the 'undercover peace-and-lover' some of us used to know."

"Nah," Zev said, looking straight ahead. "This is real-politik. Hardcore."

The muezzin had stopped praying. They couldn't even hear the soldiers laughing at their checkpoints.

"Listen to the quiet," Zev said. "It's nuclear quiet. Real spooky. Take this," he said, reaching into his belt and pulling out a .38 Special.

"No way," Eli said. "I don't need this." Zev had offered Eli the gun before, but he had always been afraid to take it.

"You do," Zev said. "I mean you really need something with a cartridge out here. This is the OK Corral, man. Injun country."

Eli handed it back to Zev. The last time he had held a gun was the night *Spy, Berliner* was canceled. He was drunk and had taken it from the set and brought it home. He wore the long-nosed opera mask on his face and fired blanks at his wife as she ran screaming out the back door.

Zev pressed the .38 back into Eli's hands and slung his Uzi around into his own hands. He smiled. "God created the universe and this is the instrument of his will. Do you have earplugs?"

"No," Eli said. "I'm not taking this."

"Always carry earplugs, boychick," Zev said, ignoring Eli, brushing back his sidecurls, his graying peyot, as he slipped the plugs into his ears. He gave a pair to Eli, who did the same. "This is target practice," he said. "Do you see the water tanks on top of the houses?" He marched ahead up a steep potholed street as he cocked his gun. Water tanks, solar heaters, and TV antennas rose out of the rooftops in a chaotic mess. The air was just cold enough that Eli could see his breath moving ahead of him in the dark. He knew now that he would follow Zev anywhere.

Zev gave him the thumbs-up sign and said, "Let's kick out the jams."

And then pop, Pop, POP, from Zev's gun, as he ran, firing at rooftops and whooping like an Indian. Eli held the gun at his side and ran to keep up with Zev, who continued shooting at the tanks, the odd shot answered with a metallic ping.

They stopped for a breath at the crest of a hill where Zev coughed and spat phlegm on the ground. From the next street over they could hear Israeli soldiers barking Hebrew orders into a megaphone. Blue siren lights strafed across the run-down buildings, as army patrol jeeps squealed around the corner from both directions and a half-dozen soldiers jumped out, shouting at them in Hebrew. Eli tried to run, flinging his gun to the ground, but a short Russian soldier with a bullet-shaped head in a red beret jammed his gun into Eli's chest and pushed him against a wall. Another soldier did the same to Zev. They spoke quickly in Hebrew. Eli didn't understand a word.

"Just show them your ID," Zev said. "No big deal. You'll understand real fast that there are two laws in the wild West Bank: one for us and one for the Arabs."

The tallest soldier addressed them in English. He wore oval-shaped glasses and Eli thought he looked like an arrogant prick. "You come to Israel because you are a Jew and you act like a maniac. Tell me, why is it that all of the scum of the world comes to Israel? You have a home in Brooklyn or Miami, no? You are a Zionist? Good. Go to Jeruzalem," he said, pronouncing the "s" as a "z." "We don't want to fight for Hevron."

"We're just living on the land of the Jewish people," Eli said. The short Russian pressed himself hard against Eli's chest. He had a gold front tooth.

"You don't have to tell these assholes anything," Zev said, picking the .38 up off the ground and handing it to Eli.

"Where are you going with your girlfriend?" the soldier asked Zev.

"Can't a Jew walk down the street without being hassled?" Zev said.

"Trust me. The Messiah will not come any faster if you stay in Hevron," the soldier said, smiling. He lit a cigarette and offered one to each of them. "Since you did not shoot anyone, you can go. But be quiet. There is a curfew. Go straight home. And put your guns away. Leave the killing to the army."

The Russian soldier backhanded Eli in the face, bloodying his nose, before jumping into the jeep and driving off. The streets were quiet again. Zev spat onto the ground and whispered, "Fucking brownshirts."

Eli patted Zev on the shoulder as if to say, "It's okay." He still had the .38 in his hand. He aimed it down the empty street and cocked the trigger. The hammer fell and white fire burst from the barrel as the chamber emptied. It was as if Eli were underwater, the sound muffled by his earplugs. He fired his gun until it was empty, and then he and Zev hammered at windows, cars, and anything else in their path as they made their way back home.

Eli led his sheep down from the hills and into a dried-out wadi. He caught a glimpse at himself in the blade of his knife and he was wild-haired and dirty, and was ashamed in the presence of the gray wolf.

"I'm sorry," he said to the wolf. "You are so beautiful. I know God is in you. How can I get more of God in me?"

The wolf was silent.

Eli clipped his fingernails and toenails, cut his itching hair to the scalp, wrapped a white sheet around his body, fraying the corners, and wound a dirty shirt around his head like a turban, all the time repeating: "I believe with complete faith that the Creator blessed is his name knows all the deeds and thoughts of human beings. I believe with complete faith the Creator blessed is his name rewards with goodness all those that observe his commandments and punishes those who violate his commandments. I believe with complete faith in the coming of the Messiah and even though he may delay I anticipate every day that he will come."

When Eli prayed, he was talking to God. When he meditated he listened. And after a while if he listened carefully, his head would tighten and God would say, "You are doing all right," or "I will call for you when it is time."

A shepherd can't sit still, Eli figured, especially when he is seeking the Almighty. And the soldiers may return, he thought. So he hefted his load onto his shoulders and wandered. With the sun rising in his face, he wandered to the east with his sheep, crossing the main highway south of Beit Lechem. His pack seemed to lighten as he zigzagged back and forth between the villages and settlements, never stopping for hospitality, prodding his flock onward. East of Tekoa on the edge of the Judean wilderness, the blue sky turned dark with hundreds of black storks flying overhead, their red stomachs winking between their flapping wings.

The desert rolled like women before him, naked and round, lounging in the sun. He saw spread legs, bare breasts, and long arched necks. He even saw the hurt face of his wife but pushed it from his mind. It was like the very landscape before him was a relief map of his past. He huddled close to his sheep for warmth.

One morning, he awoke to find that the wolf had taken one of his sheep and torn it apart, leaving the carcass for him to find, slashed apart upon a large flat stone. A sign, Eli thought.

He knew it was time now to atone for his sins. He laid his bag on the ground and dug in the earth with his hands, pulled up rocks and boulders, and carried them to the highest spot he could find. He prepared an altar of stone, bound the healthiest sheep he could find on the altar, and cried out to God that he would never sin again. He thought of the binding of Isaac, the ultimate act of faith, and thought: If I were Abraham, I would not have had the faith to bring my son to Mount Moriah, the way Abraham had been told to do with Isaac. He could not imagine tying up his son, prepared to slash his throat. What if God did not stop him?

I am not a good father, Eli thought, I am not a good father. And then he thought of his own weak father who had survived the Holocaust, gone to synagogue on the sly, and put up Christmas lights every winter. His father used to say, "the Jews are the chosen people, chosen to suffer." He just didn't get it, Eli thought. His father hadn't understood what a gift it is to be a Jew.

Eli shouted out, "For the master race!" as he slashed the throat of the long-eared sheep. And it was so serene as he grabbed a handful of its beige coat in his fist and cut back across its throat with a penknife. He poured the blood on the altar and burned the flesh, and the smell was heavenly, like a divine barbecue. When the flesh was charred and hard, he ate it and felt closer to God, felt the burned offering become part of him.

Eli and Zev walked every night through the empty city during the curfew. The air was still cool and damp, and they splashed through puddles, laughing through the streets.

They reached a dark alley at the edge of town, then plunged down a slope into an Arab vineyard. Eli followed close behind Zev, heard his feet stick and unstick in the mud, his gun swaying as he moved.

"Rabbi Kahane goes to Heaven and meets God who invites him to dinner," Zev said, chopping his arm up and down for emphasis. "God introduces the rabbi to the other guests, 'This is Jesus Christ, this is Moses, this is Buddha.' Kahane shakes their hands and sits down."

Eli caught up to Zev, laughing. He had told this exact same joke to some yeshiva students the day before. "The soup comes and there's no spoon. 'God,' says the rabbi, 'I don't have a spoon.' God looks over his shoulder, snaps his fingers and calls . . ."

"Muhammad," Eli burst in, "you forgot the spoons!"

They reached the barbed-wire fence surrounding the Jewish settlement of Kiryat Arba, which was known throughout Israel as being a hotbed for Jewish extremism. But to Eli and Zev, it was just a suburb of Hebron, a bedroom community with neat rows of whitewashed villas, TV antennas, solar panels, and clean, quiet streets.

Zev worked part-time in the falafel stand by the city's entrance and knew the guard by name. "Shalom," Zev called to the guard.

"Zevic! *Ma nish ma?*"

"*Yala!* Open up, Yossi. There's Arabs out here."

The guard was one of those big-bellied Yemenite men one might see at soccer games, shouting and waving their thick arms. His *tzitzis* hung sloppily from his pants and his blue knitted *kippah* almost covered his bald spot. He tossed newspapers into an oil-drum bonfire as he spoke about the curfew in a slow guttural English.

"Vis-à-vis the closure. It is our only tactic," Yossi said.

"When they kill Jews, people on the street, what can you do? We are in a militantic struggle with the Arabs." Yossi paused while he closed the gate. "But Jews don't antagonate. Everything here is only about security."

"*Baruch Hashem*," Eli said. "Security. Then peace."

"This peace," Zev added, "is a peace of shit."

"You're here to see Doctor Goldstein?" Yossi asked.

Zev had been friends with Goldstein and had been his next-door neighbor for more than a year. Now he continued to visit him twice a week. Eli had been in a bar in the East Village when he heard about the massacre on the news: twenty-nine Palestinians killed during prayer at the Cave of the Patriarchs, almost two hundred injured. He had seen the sprawled bodies and hysterical widows and mothers on his television, but he didn't understand at the time that Baruch Goldstein was a hero, like Judah Maccabee, or Samson.

His resting place lay in a municipal park at the entrance of the city, not a mile away from where he was murdered by the angry mob. They walked in silence along the stone promenade until they reached the grave. Eli had not gone to his own father's funeral or visited the grave. And every time Eli made the stroll along the stone promenade, he could feel the blood slowing in his veins, his mouth dry, his head pulsing, as if a wire had been tightened around his skull.

They reached a giant block of polished stone engraved in Hebrew. There were benches on either side, a cabinet full of prayer books, and a sink for hand washing. Zev blew some smoke into the air with a deep breath, grabbed a prayer book, and began to sway in silent worship. Eli walked over to the cabinet and pulled out a leather-bound book. Just beyond, he could see the outlines of rough boulders and twisted weeds and plants, and farther beyond, the blue flashing light of an army patrol jeep driving along the Hebron Road.

A cold wind swirled around them out there on the edge of town unprotected by trees or buildings. Eli could barely hear Zev's prayer above the wind, which he was sure was God's breathing. But he joined in, repeating the words he had said so many times since he had come to Hebron:

> *Blessed are You, Adonai,*
> *our God and God of our fathers,*
> *God of Abraham, God of Isaac, God of Jacob,*
> *Great, mighty, and awesome God,*
> *Highest God and Doer of good, kind deeds,*
> *Master of all,*
> *Who remembers the love of the Patriarchs*
> *and brings a redeemer to their children's children*
> *for His name's sake with love.*
> *King, Helper, Rescuer, and Shield.*
> *Blessed are You, Adonai, Shield of Abraham*

Zev was wailing, crying out to the sky, sobbing, as he shook his fist at the starry sky.

"What's the matter?" Eli asked.

Tears poured down Zev's face into his beard.

Zev sniffled above his prayer book. "You know, man, we have these places everywhere where someone died, these little, like, shrines." He paused and closed his prayer book. "Do you know why I came to Israel?"

"Because you're a Jew," Eli said.

"Jerusalem," he said. "*Ye-ru-sha-lay-im*. City of Peace. Believe it or not, I thought that was so beautiful. I was into peace and I just got on a plane one day with my rucksack. But you can't be into peace here, people look at you like they want to put you away, they say 'what do you mean, "peace"?' Reality poisons you, you just look around and everywhere there is violence and hatred and brutality. On the buses, on the street, people will kill you if you take their parking spot. Forget about the Arabs, there's nowhere else in the world where Jews are hated so much by other Jews. Everybody's fighting here. Everybody's at war."

"Zev," Eli said. "Let's go home."

He took Zev's arm in his, but instead of him straightening up, Zev threw his arms around Eli and continued to sob. His hot breath tickled Eli's ear, the way his boy's breath had the last time he saw him.

I'm not strong enough for this, Eli thought. And he began to cry, too. His throat felt thick and his body trembled as he grabbed tighter hold of Zev.

"He was my friend," Zev said.

"I'm your friend, too," Eli said.

"I know, man. You don't have to cry."

"I can't help it," Eli said. "I was just thinking."

"It's okay," Zev said. "He's in a better place now."

Eli pulled away from Zev. The tears in his eyes made everything seem double. "I'm not crying about a killer."

"He wasn't a killer," Zev said, stiffening. "He was a doctor, a fine doctor. He didn't just go down there and say, 'It's time to kill Arabs.'"

"I'm sorry," Eli said. "I shouldn't have . . ."

"He saved people's lives, man." Zev paused, and shook his head in disgust. "I remember the day of the massacre, when I heard about the massacre at the Cave of Machpelah, I was so thankful that it wasn't Jews who were killed."

"I'm thinking about my family," Eli said.

"You're with your family," Zev said.

Eli could see the blue lights of an army jeep moving in the distance.

"Do you know, after that horrible last night at home," Eli said, "I went on a six-month bender, ended up lost in the subways without a wallet or shoes. I don't even know how I got to my mother's place. She wouldn't even look at me."

"Let's go home," Zev said, offering a tissue to Eli.

"No," Eli said. "Josh should have his bar mitzvah soon."

"He's not even Jewish," Zev said. "His mother's not a Jew."

"I don't know if they'll ever speak to me again."

"Forget it," Zev said. "Keep on keepin' on. We'll find you a real wife, a Jewish wife."

"But, I loved —" Eli started to say.

"You didn't love anyone. Now, listen and listen good. It's not the same. Not even close," Zev said. "That is your goyish little family. This man is a major player in Jewish history we're talking about."

Each day Eli's flock became smaller. He wandered back and forth, both against the sun and toward it, not bothering any longer to prepare an altar for each sacrifice. Sometimes he tore at the sheep with his bare hands and they screamed like crying infants. He ate the flesh raw and wore the skins on his back, or stuffed them into his bag. He prayed hard and waited for an answer. A nauseating hunger tore through his stomach and he thought, "The closer you get to God, the faster and harder you get smacked. But I am getting closer."

He stared at the full moon, at the curve of its edges pulsing against an endless night sky and it was as if he was gazing into the eye of God. He prayed with fury for hours, shaking and calling out to the sky, "I am dust, and there is nothing lower than dust." Sweat began to pour down his face and he cried out, "Don't you understand me?" He buried his face in the rough wool of his pack and wept.

Eli thought he heard a child's voice calling him and he woke up clinging to his pack. The moon was at the top of the sky now and lit the hillsides with a brilliant silvery glow. Then he heard it: "Eli Israel, son of man."

"Hello!" Eli called.

He heard thousands of wings flapping near him, and then closer still. He leaped to his feet and jumped up and down, batting at his head as if a swarm of bees had flown into his ears and were working their way into his brain. A flash of color filled his eyes, a prism of colors that he had never seen before. All the organs of his body began to tremble and he was sure he was going to die, as excrement and urine and vomit poured out of him.

"You are purified," a voice said at last. "Go to the mountain. Go to Jerusalem and speak my words."

"You need to find a wife," Zev said to Eli one day. "A Jewish wife."

He had been with Zev for nearly a year and had spent most of his time studying. Eli had not thought of women in a long time. "It says in the Torah you're only half a person if you're not married."

"But, you're not married," Eli said.

"I'm not ready yet. But you, my friend, have come so far."

It was true. Eli could quote the Torah, the Talmud, the Zohar, and other texts as if he had been studying for years.

"I know a rabbi in Jerusalem. Rabbi Lev, the Love Rabbi. I'm sure he can arrange a *shiduch*."

"Why haven't you gone to see him?" Eli asked.

"I have, man. But it was a disaster," Zev said. "One was a Moroccan widow with six kids who could cook couscous with chicken that melted from the bone and knew Torah left to right and right to left, but I didn't want to get tangled up with someone else's children, if you know what I mean? Another wanted to move to Brooklyn to wait for a sign from the Lubavitcher rebbe, but I'm not going back to Babylon, man. Listen, some didn't even speak English. Could you imagine smearing the language of the Torah, to order McDonald's cheeseburgers, to buy toilet paper, to discuss the weather? It was a total disaster. That only proves that I'm not ready. But you," Zev said, embracing Eli in a warm bear hug, "you have achieved *tschuva,* redemption."

Eli felt his stomach drop and he thought of Kate and Josh and how things had fallen apart. "No. I'm not ready."

"Yeah, man, you are. You're, like, fucking clean. A clean slate."

"Do you remember when the show went off the air, *Spy, Berliner*? And I told you I got drunk and came home from the set wearing that long-nosed opera mask, with a pistol and fired blanks at Kate, just scared the hell out of her. And I really thought Josh was out on a sleepover. So the whole thing started as a joke."

Zev nodded his head and smiled. Eli could see him absently fingering the handle of his pistol.

"Well, I didn't tell you that after she ran out, I just started bawling. Like I knew that I was on the edge of a really deep pit, and I was crying and crying, I thought I was such a schmuck, you know I was messing around with every guest star on the show and Kate must have known. I was feeling sorry for myself, and she slipped in through the screen door and came over and put her arms around me." Eli wiped a tear from his eye with his finger and then slid the finger into his mouth. "She put her arms around me and said it'll be all right or something, and this is *after* I fired the gun at her. And then I just snapped, I was still wearing that ugly mask, I don't know what I was thinking, I just sort of threw her on the floor and started to, started to . . ."

Eli took a deep breath, but couldn't get enough air.

"I know, man," Zev said. "But she was your wife, that's part of the deal."

"No!" Eli shouted suddenly. "With the fucking nose. That's how I did it, maybe I thought it would be fun, or different, and I know now I was hurting her, it was like I was nodding my head, yes, yes, yes, into her as she was saying no, no, no. And then the kid walks in, and she starts screaming bloody murder, 'Get out! Get out of my house.' And that was it."

"Hey, man. Don't sweat it. God forgives you."

"It was awful. You should have seen his face. He didn't know what his father was doing with that mask. But he saw his mother curled up on the floor like a wounded kitten or something."

"Hey," Zev said. "It's over. You paid for it. God knows you did. That's what counts. You're even-steven, now."

A few days later Eli called to speak with Rabbi Lev.

"Eli," Rabbi Lev said, with his Brooklyn accent. "I found your *beshert*. A terrific girl. A regular Bess Myerson. Come to Jerusalem and meet her."

Beneath a steady rain, Eli Israel dug in the rocky earth with his penknife and then with his hands, until he had grooved out a shallow pit. His hands were raw and bloody and he lifted the bag he had fashioned from the old riding blanket and tossed it into the groove in the earth. He hastily covered it as he mumbled Kaddish.

He walked all afternoon before reaching a highway, and continued, warmed by his thoughts. He felt light and his groin pulsed. He allowed himself to think about having a woman again without fear, knowing that he was pure of mind and spirit. "Children," he thought. "Imagine, one for each tribe of Israel: Judah, Levi, Gad, Asher, Binyamin, Zevulun, Reuven, Naphtali, Simeon, Dan, Issachar, Joseph, all of them populating the land." Eli smiled. He thought of returning to Rabbi Lev, but knew he could find his own woman now.

When he finally reached Jerusalem, his feet were raw and bruised and he thought of what it says in the Talmud: that of the ten portions of beauty in the world, nine were deposited in Jerusalem. He arrived late that night and was stunned to see the city, as if seeing it for the first time. Across the darkness, buried in the mountains, floating in the sky, surrounded by hills were the walls of a city that was like a dream. Jerusalem was almost there, and almost not, more spirit than stone, a ghost against the sky, domes and towers climbing straight to heaven.

Eli thought of Zev back in Hebron and wondered if they would soon meet again. He smiled and took a deep breath, remembering what Zev had said about going up to Jerusalem: "You are going into the eye of the hurricane, man, the tip of the arrow, the top of the mountain. How can you not feel like one of God's angels?"

The first morning light seemed to rise out of the stones themselves. As he walked down into the Hinnom Valley he saw silhouettes of trees and bushes and heard bells peal across the gray sky, and voices from all around, wailing, echoing through the valley. Then, still silence. Nothing moved at all and a pink blush spread from the east into the full colors of morning, then a brilliant white sun, huge palm trees, and the vaulted entrance of Jaffa Gate.

Eli felt as if he was two thousand years old, three thousand even. He felt as if he had just been born. In the month of Nisan in the year 5756, Eli entered Jerusalem prepared to bring the Messiah at last to Israel and the Jewish people.

Eli borrowed Zev's car for the last time as he drove up to Jerusalem to meet his *beshert*. He had to drive through Halhul, a dusty Arab village, and always gunned his engine through to the main highway. He knew the Arab urchins along the road could pick out yellow Israeli plates from a mile away and sometimes threw stones at cars as they passed.

The radio was turned up loud, tuned to a pirate station that played American music. Eli had almost made it by the vegetable stands and the last cluster of houses at the edge of town when he saw a group of boys gathered at the side of the road. He pressed the gas harder, just as they started hurling stones at his car. One of the boys slingshotted a fist-sized stone that smashed his window, cracking a huge spiderweb on Eli's windshield. Eli tried to turn the car away as a second volley of stones flew at it, but the car skidded into a ditch, nearly spinning completely around. With the car stuck in the ditch, Eli suddenly realized how bright the sun was and how his eyes hurt. At first Eli began to pray, terrified now that with his car idle another kid might launch a Molotov cocktail at him. He'd seen Jewish cars burned up at the side of the road before, and he reached into the glove compartment and grabbed his .38. Eli jumped out of the car. Most of the kids had scattered into the narrow side streets, but Eli could see a young Arab boy riding away on a donkey, calling, *"Itbah al-Yahud,"* "kill the Jew."

Everything became quiet for a moment as he drew his pistol. The whole world seemed to be frozen in that blazing white light. All he could think was *never again, never again, never again, never again, never again*. Then, total clarity. The sort of locked-in feeling he had felt during prayer. No sound, smell, taste. Nothing. Just the visual, intense, superreal, a tunnel of light and colors from him to the boy.

Eli fired until the gun was empty and dropped the kid into the dirt at the side of the road. It seemed to take forever for the bullets to reach him and then the bright yellow dust came up all around him and Eli was back in the world. The boy's donkey skittered off as Eli reached into his utility vest pocket for more bullets. His hands shook and he could only press two bullets into the gun, dropping the rest onto the ground. The boy lay still at the side of the road. He was dead, Eli knew that right away. His ears rang with a high-pitched hum as he walked toward the boy with the gun still in his hand.

Lying there in the dirt the boy looked so young, no more than thirteen, Eli thought. He could have been his kid. He smelled of sweat and still wore a backward smile and the first hints of a mustache on his face. Eli brushed his hand through his brown hair and closed his own eyes. For a moment, he saw the darkness of his eyelids and wondered, *"Is this what death looks like?"*

One of the bullets had come out the boy's chest and another had gone in his shoulder. Eli pushed the body over with his foot so he wouldn't have to look at him anymore.

The boy's red, black, and green riding blanket lay crumpled on the ground not five feet from him. Eli picked it up and shook out the dust. He wrapped the thick blanket around the boy, who was bleeding furiously from the chest and mouth.

The boy wasn't very heavy, maybe eighty or ninety pounds, like a small deer. He could have lifted the boy's weight three times over. And for a moment, he remembered carrying Josh with a fever of a hundred and three, up the stairs to his room, and laying him on his bed.

The boy's bare feet dangled from the blanket, slapping together as Eli walked. There was no one around — no Arabs, no Jews, no one. Not even the sound of a distant car engine to break the silence. It seemed to Eli that even God had winked and turned his back at that moment. He felt nothing carrying the boy back to Zev's car, as if he weren't even there but only imagining the whole scene. Somewhere in the distance black smoke rose into the sky where the local Arabs burned garbage.

Eli opened the trunk and threw the boy in next to the spare tire. The blanket covered his face but his body was twisted in a strange way. Eli closed the trunk, and for a moment his head spun, like it was being ripped open from the inside. He opened the trunk again and placed the boy inside the blanket and wrapped it twice around him, covering him completely.

He got into the car and prayed, hoping the engine would start before anyone returned. And the car revved and pulled itself out of the ditch and back onto the road. The radio was blaring Presley's "Blue Moon of Kentucky." Eli turned the volume down and opened the glove compartment. He tossed in his pistol, and pulled out an old pair of Zev's mirrored sunglasses.

"God teaches you hard," Eli thought, putting the glasses on. "These things happen on the road to redemption, on the road to Jerusalem. But God forgives you for what you do and I love Him."

For as Long as the Lamp Is Burning

THE WEEK BEFORE, Avshalom Cohen and his aging mother, Miriam, sat drinking tea together in her Rehavia apartment. It was summer, and violin music played through the trees and gardens outside the open kitchen window. In the next building Mr. Herzog scratched out the music that had saved his life at Auschwitz with a deeper sadness than usual, his arthritic hands fumbling across the strings, the bow just missing the right note. Miriam Cohen told her son that Mr. Herzog had fallen on Azza Street on his way home from the *shuk* and had refused, as he had his whole life, to visit a doctor. He was finally ready to meet his wife again in the Great Beyond.

"Such nonsense," Miriam said. "I know my Hershel is not waiting for me. He has gone to dust and there he will stay."

"Momma," Avshalom said for the thousandth time. "Of course Poppa is waiting for you."

"That's why he has written my name across the stars," she said bitterly. "He has forgotten me, left me behind. I will never forget. Never forget."

Avshalom knew that another one of her crying fits was coming on — whenever she said she would never forget, she wept, tore at her hair, waved her tattooed left arm in her son's face, cursed at him.

"You were such a good boy, Avshi. As good, maybe, as your brother and sister. And then you left me, too, and moved to Mevaseret with the Sephardi school teacher."

"It is only a twenty-minute drive," he said, ignoring the jab at his wife.

"You never visit," she said. "The only visitors I have are the gestapo and their black dogs gnashing their teeth when I try and sleep."

"Momma, don't talk that way. Put it out of your mind."

"Never!" she said. "I don't sleep anymore. They are in my room. I can hear them whispering. Last night, I woke up and could not breathe and I went to the kitchen and someone had snuck in and turned on the gas. I could have died. I couldn't breathe."

"It was just bad dreams and your emphysema," Avshalom said.

"I have no such thing. I can't even pronounce the word. I'm telling you, the Nazi Arabs came to my home. They move things when I am not looking so I can't find them."

He placed his hand on her veined, shaking hand. "Momma, I'm going to leave now."

"Leave!" she said. And then, all at once, Mr. Herzog's lugubrious playing came to an abrupt end.

Avshalom's telephone rang sometime after midnight. He was in bed with his wife, Shira. She picked up the phone.

"Avshi, your mother."

"Hello, Momma," he said, taking up the telephone.

Her voice was thin and scared on the other end of the phone. "Where were you when I called?"

"We were only in Eilat with the boys for a couple of days."

"You must come over. The Nazis, they are here again."

"But Momma," he said.

"Did I give you the last milk of my breast?" she asked.

He hung up the phone and turned to Shira, softly kissing her cheek.

"Sad dreams?" Shira asked.

"Another one of her fits," he said.

When he arrived at his mother's home, Avshalom found her standing in the door of her apartment brandishing a worn slipper in her hand.

"Hurry, Avshi, hurry!" she called as he got out of his car.

"How are you feeling, Momma?"

"The Nazis," she cried. "They were here."

He climbed the stairs slowly, his tiny mother waving her slipper to speed him up.

"You heard Mr. Herzog died," she said.

"No," Avshalom said, taking his mother's soft hand. She wore a brown cardigan sweater over her cotton nightgown. She squeezed his hand tightly.

"He died and stayed in his home for three days before someone found him."

"He was a nice man," Avshalom said.

"And look where that got him," she said.

His mother's usually immaculate apartment was a mess: plates were piled in the sink; papers lay everywhere, on the floor, the table, the sofa; the curtains were pulled closed; the room smelled stale; even his father's study, a model of German order, was a testament to chaos — his large leather-bound books had been pulled from their shelves and strewn about; his ashtray that had lain full for the last eight years since his death had been turned over on his desk; his banker's lamp lay smashed and broken.

She had always been neat in the German tradition. She once joked with Avshalom as a child that if he went out to play after dinner without brushing his teeth and *has v'chalila* he died in an attack, she promised to pry open his coffin with her stirring ladle to clean his teeth for the journey.

"What happened, Momma?" Avshalom said, surveying the damage.

She threw the slipper at him, missing his head by a few feet. "I told you, the Nazis came and took things."

He pulled his mother close to him and held her in his arms, an embrace so warm he hoped it would chase away every phantasm until Judgment Day. She, too, carried an odd smell about her, a smell of age and neglect that he had never noticed before. She pulled herself violently from his arms.

"I made a prayer for him."

"Who?" Avshalom asked.

"Good-bye, Mr. Herzog. Good-bye."

"Momma. What happened?"

"Like *Kristallnacht,*" she said. "They even took my mezuzah from the front doorpost."

She began to cry, quiet at first, her lip trembling, then from the depths of her body she burst out weeping. "My beautiful mezuzah!" She swung her arms and struck out at her son. "I will never forget."

Why would somebody steal his mother's mezuzah? Avshalom wondered. He went to the door and could see the outline, slanting inward at the top of the doorpost, where the mezuzah had been for more than forty years. It had been pried off, that much he could tell. And it was a beautiful piece, crafted in Weimar Germany, a time when Jews enjoyed a brief renaissance before the yellow stars and cattle cars.

Two portions of the Torah from Deuteronomy inside the silver case, gone. "HEAR O ISRAEL: THE LORD OUR GOD. THE LORD IS ONE," he repeated to himself in Hebrew, running his fingers over the bare space on the door. "You shall write these words on the doorposts of your house." Why would someone steal an old woman's mezuzah? He remembered as a child being too short to reach it, kissing his fingertips and touching them to the doorpost beneath the shining silver. And later, when he had grown, he could finally see the intricate carving: flowers blooming at the top and the bottom, a jeweled crown, and tiny silver doors like a miniature ark, revealing on its parchment when opened the holy name *Shaddai.* What a mystical thrill he had felt, repeating that name as a youth, an all-powerful name that was older than any tree or building or person he knew.

"I know who took it," his mother said.

"Who?" Avshalom said, closing the door and leading his mother back into the living room.

"The man who plants the flowers and fixes the garden. He is a Nazi Arab. I have seen him. He took my mezuzah. The Nazi took it."

"Dudu took your mezuzah?"

"Yes. Yes. Dudu took it."

"Dudu is Jewish," Avshalom said. "Why would he take it?"

"No, no," she cried. "He is not Jewish. I have seen him riding his donkey and goose-stepping on the street. He is the one. He took it."

"Sit down, Momma."

"It hurts my bones to sit. I will stand."

"Sit down, Momma," he said, clearing a space on the couch.

She sat, and slid the sleeves of her brown cardigan up her arm, revealing the blue numbers burned into her skin.

"Momma, I am sure Dudu did not take the mezuzah."

"Oh, you are sure," she said. "The laborer from Mevaseret has all the answers now. Tell me, Rashi: Why is the grass blue? Why is the moon made of Limburger cheese?"

"Stop it, Momma."

"You are lucky you were not at the camps. You would not have survived like your father and I. You are too believing. Poor Avshi, if the Nazis had told you to go to the showers, you would have run there smiling with a towel and shampoo in your hands."

They sat in silence. Avshalom seethed. For a moment, he wanted to strike his mother, dash her broken to the floor like a rag doll.

"Momma?"

"Son of mine," she answered.

"What's wrong?"

"And to think you were the smart one. I told you, the Nazis took my mezuzah."

"Did you go to Mr. Herzog's funeral?"

"Achh!" she said. "Funerals. I have been to too many. After your father, I never went to another. What good is it?"

"To pay your respects."

"To the dead? You don't understand anything, do you? When your father died, I had to take everything from his life and carry it with me. Right here." She tapped her right temple with her forefinger. "And when Moses Solomon died, and when Esti Hertz died, all of them. Now I have to remember for Mr. Herzog, too."

"You miss Mr. Herzog."

"Never!" she said. "He scraped at that violin all day like a cat scratching on a pole. Miss him? No. But we are one less now. You don't understand. You live in Mevaseret with your family and you build things with your hands. You will forget me when I'm gone. Soon, there will be none of us left. Next door there are students living, and they play rock and roll music, bang, bang, bang, all the time. What do they know of anything? I am tired, Avshi. My mezuzah is gone. Your father's study is ruined."

"Momma, go to sleep."

"For what?"

"Let me tell you a story I remember from school."

"A story about car engines and grease monkeys I do not want to hear."

"There are two ships sailing on the seas."

"Ha! What do you know of that, you only know the Kinneret and the *Yam Ha Melach*."

"The ship that comes into the port is seen by the wise man as more of an object of joy than the ship about to leave the harbor."

"Not if the ship is going into Cyprus," she said. "I have been to Cyprus, you know . . ."

"Momma, listen, just because a ship is leaving the port does not mean you should be sad or afraid. Because, soon that ship will reach another harbor, a glorious harbor . . ."

"My smart boy," she said. "My smart, smart boy. You are speaking Greek." She let out a long loud yawn. "But you have found success. I will sleep now."

Avshalom stood up and helped his mother to her feet. He took her arm and led her to the bedroom. She sat on the bed and removed her brown cardigan and handed it to her son, and she got into bed.

"Do you remember what I said to you as a child when I put you to bed?"

"You said, 'goodnight.'"

"Oh, Avshi. Turn out the light. I will clean up the apartment tomorrow."

He clicked off the light, leaned over, and planted a soft kiss on her forehead. He walked out of the room with her sweater over his arm.

"*Schlaf gut, mein Kind,*" she called after him sarcastically.

Alone in his mother's living room, Avshalom began to tidy up, gathering loose papers in his arms. He still had his mother's brown sweater draped over his left arm. He hung it over a chair and then noticed a weight, something in the pocket. He reached inside and found shining in his palm his mother's Weimar mezuzah. She must have taken it down to clean it, polished it to a fine shine, and then placed it in her pocket and forgotten it.

She had turned over pillows on the sofa, pulled chairs out from the living room table, emptied her china cabinet, breaking two plates. She had entered her husband's study, ransacked the bookshelves, torn papers from his drawers, then she had gone to the kitchen — and that is where Avshalom found the soup spoon, bent and twisted from the effort of prying, on the floor beneath the kitchen table. And in the bathroom, beside the sink among tubes and pills, he found a small jar of silver polish, her toothbrush lying on the floor, its bristles tarnished and black.

He held the mezuzah tight in his hand and thought of his wife and what she would say to him: "You want your impossible mother to live with us?"

Avshalom slowed his car at the edge of the city and pulled over at the top of a valley. He stepped out of his car and walked to the edge of a steep cliff. The abandoned village of Lifta lay below. Somewhere in the darkness, a solitary horse neighed. He pulled the mezuzah from his pocket, cradled it in his two hands, and shivered against a wind. He would never tell his mother about the mezuzah. He would let her think that her mind was a steel trap and would let her live with the mystery until she stepped off the planet to meet her husband. He would give the mezuzah to his twelve-year-old, David, and he would fasten it to his door when he had a home of his own.

Avshalom looked into the black sky splashed with yellow stars and the glowing horn of the moon.

"Of course we will not forget, Momma," he whispered to himself. "Look at the stars. There are six million of them. And the moon, it is so beautiful tonight."

The King of the
King of Falafel

Mordechai HaLevi was still very young — only seventeen years old — when his father, Boaz, the King of Falafel, tried to run over his chief competitor with his rusty Toyota truck and was sentenced to three years in prison in the outskirts of Jerusalem.

The King of the King of Falafel had opened business across the busy thoroughfare of King George Street only six months earlier, undercutting the King of Falafel, selling two falafels for the price of one. Boaz told his son that Benny Ovadiah, the newly crowned king, must have been scraping vegetables off the floor of the Mahane Yehuda market and selling them in his sandwiches for such a price.

"He's using rat meat to make his shwarmas. I know it," Mordechai's father said. "How else can a man sell falafels so cheap and still keep the rain off his head?"

"Maybe the angels," Mordechai said.

"The only angel I know is the Angel of Death," his father answered, turning his wedding ring on his thick finger.

The week before his father went berserk, Mordechai was sent across the street to plead with Benny Ovadiah, who was a war hero, saved by golden-winged angels at the Allenby Bridge. He was a religious man and would listen to reason.

Manufactured air blew into Mordechai's face as he entered the gleaming oasis of polished marble and glass where twisting rams horns, bronze water pipes, and wide-eyed *hamsas* hung decorously from the walls. Hungry patrons sat in plush chairs covered with richly embroidered swirling Yemenite stitchwork beneath a sky-blue domed ceiling. They ate from round marble tables that were smoother than ice and whiter than snow. Mordechai wiped his brow, leaving the heat of King George Street behind. Pictures of the great mystics — the Baba Sali, Ovadiah Yosef, and others — were taped on the glass beside the mandate-era cash register that ka-chinged with annoying regularity.

Benny Ovadiah stood behind the counter wearing a large black *kippah* pulled low onto his forehead.

"My father wants you to move away," Mordechai said. "He is the King of Falafel."

"But, I am the King of the King of Falafel," Benny Ovadiah said, throwing a falafel ball in the air and catching it in an open pita.

He was right. His prep men juggled their falafel balls in the air, tapped their tongs on the counter, and sang *Heenay Ma' Tov* as they made their sandwiches. The King of the King of Falafel offered thirty-two different toppings, including thick hummus, zesty tahini, tomatoes, cucumbers, pickled turnips, radishes, olives, eggplant, red peppers, onions, and chips.

"Give this to your father," Benny Ovadiah said, handing Mordechai the fully dressed falafel.

"But when will you leave?" Mordechai asked.

"When the Messiah comes."

When Mordechai returned to the falafel stand to tell his father, he had to shout above the noise of the ancient ceiling fan that clattered like battling swords. His father slammed Benny Ovadiah's falafel against the wall and said, "The fucking Messiah! I'll kill him!"

Mordechai did not love falafels, but he did love his father, so he agreed to run the business while his father was away. With the help of his friend Shuki he secretly planned to drive the King of the King of Falafel out of business to honor his departed father.

Shuki was a juvenile delinquent who did not want to serve in the army and did his best to convince society that he was unfit to die in Lebanon. He wore a T-shirt that said "Rage," smoked filterless cigarettes, and spat on the street as he walked. He whispered ideas in Mordechai's ear and laughed like a sick braying beast.

They paid a Russian farmer from the north to deliver pork to Benny Ovadiah's back door, but the King of the King of Falafel could smell *treif* a mile away and threw it in the street in front of Mordechai's falafel stand. The flies buzzed above the meat all afternoon until Benny Ovadiah approached Mordechai at the end of the day as he was sweeping the floor. Only an autographed team photograph of the *Betar Yerushalayim* football club hung on the wall next to a yellowing dog-eared kashrut certificate.

"Not many customers today," Benny Ovadiah said. "The smell is difficult, the flies are worse."

"It is not so bad," Mordechai said, wondering if Benny Ovadiah smelled of body odor or cumin powder.

"You are losing money. Come and work for me. You can buy cigarettes to send your father in prison."

"I want you to leave," Mordechai said. "Go to Katamonim. We don't want you here."

"You are a punk, but there is hope for you. You honor your father even though he is a maniac. It's a commandment of God."

"But I don't love my neighbor," Mordechai said, sure now that no cumin powder in the world could smell so rank as Benny Ovadiah.

"Leave!" Mordechai shouted.

"When the Messiah comes," Benny Ovadiah said, laughing.

"There cannot be two kings of falafel."

"Why don't you call yourself the King of Shwarma, or the King of *Fuul,* or," Benny Ovadiah said in English, "the King of Fools." He grabbed his rounded belly and laughed again. "Or, maybe, the son of the King of Fools," he said, opening the door to King George Street.

To gain leverage over his enemy, Mordechai stayed open on Shabbat to take advantage of hungry tourists wandering the empty streets of Jerusalem. For a while, he did a brisk business until the black-hatted ultraorthodox from Mea Shearim caught wind of it and pelted stones and bags of dung at his falafel stand.

"Go back to Germany and destroy the sabbath," they shouted.

Cars packed with families arrived from as far away as Nahariya, Afula, and Yeroham to savor the delights of Benny Ovadiah's King of the King of Falafel.

"What spell has he put on them?" Mordechai wondered. "What angel watches over him?"

Even his most loyal customer, Reuven the Watcher, walked away from the King of Falafel saying, "Your falafel tastes like sand. I wouldn't feed it to the dead."

Mordechai gave away free samples, concocted the fruit falafel, painted a new bright red sign, shouted down his adversary through a megaphone, and continued to lose business to Benny Ovadiah. He even considered calling himself the King of the King of the King of Falafel, but did not have enough space on his tiny storefront.

Shuki suggested they steal the pita bread that was delivered to Benny Ovadiah's front door hours before the King of the King of Falafel opened for business.

"Falafel without pita is like the Dead Sea without salt," Shuki said.

They were amazed to discover that without his pitas, the King of the King of Falafel did not fold up and blow away. He thrived, in fact. People lined up all along the street, jockeyed for position, and shouted across to Mordechai and his empty stand. Finally a policeman on horseback arrived to calm the crowd, but he too dismounted and joined the hungry line.

"What's going on?" Mordechai shouted to one of the patrons.

"It's amazing," a young girl called back. "He is serving falafel on manna from heaven."

When his father wrote him asking how business was, Mordechai lied; when he asked after the nudnik who called himself 'king,' Mordechai said the filthy dog was on the run: "He's in the *mikvah* now, preparing for the Messiah."

"He should drown," his father said.

One day Shuki drank a jar of olive oil and bit into a shwarma at Benny Ovadiah's restaurant. He threw up on the floor right in front of the King of the King of Falafel and screamed, "Bad lamb! Bad lamb!"

But Benny Ovadiah had seen Shuki hanging out with Mordechai and beat him with a broom.

"Don't break your teeth. I'm not leaving," Benny Ovadiah shouted as he brought the broom down onto Shuki's head.

"What about the Messiah?" Shuki said.

"Show me the Messiah."

Frustrated and tired of falafel, they ate hamburgers at the new McDonald's, where Shuki tried to lighten the mood, moving the buns of his burger like the mouth of a hand puppet. "I am the red heifer. I taste better with cheese." And he bit into the burger, laughing.

"I am the pink heifer," Mordechai said, holding his burger. "Cook me some more, please."

"Stupid!" Shuki said, hitting Mordechai on the forehead with the palm of his hand. "Don't you remember from religion class in school where God told the children of Israel to purify themselves?"

"Take a shower," Mordechai said, laughing. "With soap!"

"He told them to sacrifice a red heifer, a pure red heifer without blemish or spot, because only the ashes of a red heifer can purify Jews so they can rebuild the Temple." Shuki paused and beat a drum roll on the table. "And-bring-the-Messiah-the-King-of-Israel."

"But there hasn't been a red heifer in Israel in over two thousand years," Mordechai said, remembering the mysterious passage.

"Yes," Shuki said, "that is true. But now . . ." And he began to hum, and then Mordechai joined in and they were singing, "Moshiach, Moshiach, Moshiach!"

They drove out of the city under a starless sky toward the west and the coastal plain. The air became warmer as they descended. Shuki rolled down his window and lit a cigarette. Mordechai fiddled with the radio dial as they drove, finding Jordan Radio in English, then *Arutz Sheva,* the Jewish settlers' pirate station, and finally *Galei Tzahal,* Army wave radio. They sang along in English at the top of their lungs.

"Remember when we were young?" Mordechai asked Shuki as they turned off the highway.

Shuki knew the kibbutz guard by name, because he used to hitch down every week to make out in the banana fields with a girl he'd met on a school trip to the Holocaust museum. They waved and drove by him, but they didn't stop at the girl's room, they kept going along the dirt road past the bulls kicking up dust, and on to the dairy. The air smelled of fresh cow manure and trees.

"Cows are so dumb," Mordechai said. "All they do is shit. They live in shit, they sleep in shit. . . ."

"Quiet," Shuki said. "Operation Secret Messiah."

The frightened cows moved away from them as one, their hooves rumbling against the earth. Mordechai and Shuki followed them twice around the pen under the moonless sky. The cows were brown and black and some were just brown.

"Okay," Shuki said, "let's get this one, she's stopped moving."

"She's too big," Mordechai said, laughing. "Even bigger than Tamar."

"My sister's having twins, idiot. Just grab one," Shuki answered. "Grab it by the tail."

But they couldn't catch the other cows, who kept circling around and around the pen in the darkness.

"Let's get this one before she wakes up," Mordechai said, slapping the fat sleepy cow on the rump. *"Yala!"*

It wasn't easy to get the giant brown cow into the truck. She wouldn't move after being prodded out of the pen.

When she finally did move she stepped on Mordechai's foot and then didn't move again.

"Ouch," Mordechai called. "She's on my foot."

"Punch her," Shuki said.

"What?"

"In the nose."

"No. You punch her."

"Tickle her, then," Shuki said, spitting onto the ground. "Like she's your girlfriend."

When they finally got her into the truck they covered her with a tarp and gunned the engine past the guard when his back was turned.

When they pulled back onto the highway, Mordechai and Shuki sang the song that they thought was so hilarious calling for the Messiah. "Moshiach, Moshiach, Moshiach! Ai, ai, ai, ai . . ."

"We should call her 'one million burgers,'" Mordechai said as they drove back up toward the holy city.

"She's the red heifer," Shuki said. "And I'm a blond."

In the alleyway behind the King of Falafel they slathered red paint onto the cow and worked it into her coat.

"The hairdresser at work," Mordechai said.

"If that will keep me from the army," Shuki said, kissing the cow dramatically on the forehead.

The cow stood still, big-eyed, oblivious.

It was nearly four o'clock in the morning when they led the red-painted cow across King George Street. Mordechai and Shuki were as red as the cow, their hands and faces smeared with paint. They were high from the paint fumes.

"Ai, ai ai, ai, wo-o, wo-o, wo-o . . ." Mordechai sang.

"Quiet," Shuki said.

"Jews are depending on you, big girl," Mordechai whispered. "In the morning they will wake to trumpets and flutes and harps. . . ."

"Shut up," Shuki said, leading the cow into the alleyway behind the King of the King of Falafel.

"At last the Messiah can come," Mordechai added, patting her on the head. "Isn't that right, Red?"

Not even a moo.

Shuki jimmied open the back door of Benny Ovadiah's King of the King of Falafel with a pocket knife he carried in his jeans. They had difficulty leading the beefy cow through the back door, her wet paint rubbing off against the door, but they forced her through, laughing as they went.

"Through the red door, destiny awaits," Mordechai said.

They left her standing alone in the dark, in the middle of the restaurant.

From across the street they could hear the red-painted cow rattling around in the darkness, a breaking of glass, battering against the steel shutter that said: KING OF THE KING OF FALAFEL, and then the graffito, "IS THE KING OF NOTHING." They heard hooves stamping and long, loud moos.

Mordechai imagined Benny Ovadiah's unblemished marble tables shattering on the floor, his tapestries trod upon, his bronze *tchotchkes* battered and stomped on. He imagined the Lubavitcher rebbe climbing out of the photo from beside the mandate-era register to sweep the cluttered floor muttering lamentations, and the frightened cow nuzzling close, dripping snot on the black-clad rabbi.

From the time they locked the cow inside, there was not

a moment of silence. Afraid that the paint fumes had made her crazy as a bull, they agonized all night under the moonless sky, without a star to wish on.

"You go see her," Mordechai said.

"No! You!"

"She's destroying the place."

"She's destroying the place," Shuki repeated, and they both broke out laughing.

Mordechai's insides heaved as he laughed and he felt a warm glow inside him. He laughed so hard he could not tell if sweat or tears poured down his face.

For a moment before the sun rose, the sky filled with stars and then morning burst out of the east to greet them.

Things were not so hilarious by the time Benny Ovadiah arrived to open the King of the King of Falafel. Both Mordechai and Shuki were exhausted and a little afraid.

"Caught with red hands," Shuki said, but he did not laugh.

The sun was out now, and there was nowhere for the two boys to hide. They stood by the side of the road and could hear Benny Ovadiah screaming and cursing, calling them sons of whores, sons of bitches, sons of shit. Mordechai turned to Shuki and offered a prayer for his soul. He was only half joking.

When Benny Ovadiah emerged from his battered restaurant, he was completely red, covered in paint or blood or both.

He carried a bloody butcher knife in his shaking hand. "You had better hope the Messiah comes now," Benny Ovadiah shouted, stepping into the street. "Then, the dead can rise again. And you will be the first."

"You can't kill us," Mordechai said.

"Why not? I can share a cell with your father."

He reached the sidewalk and grabbed Mordechai by the hair.

"It was just a joke," Mordechai said, almost in tears.

"I've slaughtered your joke," Benny Ovadiah boomed.

"But, we're neighbors," Mordechai said, the words almost swallowed. "Look," he said, pointing to the pathetic sight of Benny Ovadiah's ruined falafel restaurant across the street.

"No! Look!" Shuki cried, wide-eyed.

And, from behind an overturned table, Mordechai saw a little red calf stumble unsteadily out of the wreckage, its legs buckling like a drunk, as it mooed and stepped out to join the morning traffic.

Lucky Eighteen

Elijah's Cup

V ERY EARLY ON THE MORNING of his twenty-third birthday, Stuart Kravetz and his friend Shawn Silver stepped out of a misty rain and through a rusty ornamented gate, into the subterranean gloom and smoke of Elijah's Cup. They stepped down three stone stairs, careful not to slip on splashes of beer or vomit as they ducked their heads below an iron pipe, Kravetz holding on for balance. Shawn smiled at every face he met. He wore a light meter and camera around his neck and carried a silver briefcase in his left hand and a suitcase in his right. He wore a stylish black linen suit and a small ponytail that seemed grossly out of place for both the Holy City and Elijah's Cup. But Kravetz remembered that Shawn always dressed to travel, whether it was a road trip to Boston or a plane flight across the world. The room was filled with barefoot English travelers, blond Swedish tourists, wayward rabbinical students, wild-eyed mystics, mustached Palestinian laborers, broad-shouldered U.N. troopers, Russian whores, and bullshitters of all political stripes pounding back cheap Israeli beer, hummus, and olives.

Kravetz had not seen Shawn since leaving for Israel six months earlier, and besides having grown a goatee that covered his cleft chin, he also seemed to have gained weight. Kravetz noticed that Shawn's face seemed somehow harder, and though he was only a year older than Kravetz, he looked dried out and bloated at the same time.

The prime minister had been buried on Mount Herzl that morning, and after a long day Kravetz had gone to bed early, with his radio tuned to *Galei Tzahal* playing mournful music from the darkness. The telephone woke him at midnight. "Happy birthday, kid," the familiar voice said. "How about a drink?"

Kravetz was silent and clicked on his bedside lamp.

"I'm at the airport, brother," his old friend, Shawn Silver, said, sounding more nasal than usual. "Meet me outside Elijah's Cup in an hour."

And now they were under the smoky dome of Elijah's Cup, passing old Ministry of Tourism posters for Tiberias, Eilat, and the Dead Sea tacked to the wall. A dustpan-sized ceramic *hamsa* hung behind the bar, the shape of a hand, a dreamy blue eye centered in its palm to ward off evil. Faded photos of rabbis — a hawk-nosed Baba Sali, a turbaned Ovadiah Yosef, and other Sephardi mystics — were taped to the mirror behind the bar. A stained and tattered petition sat on the bar; the bar's owner had been caught with drugs in the Sinai, and was currently serving twenty-five years in an Egyptian prison. A wooden barrel of black olives stood nearby; customers dipped their hands in and sometimes spat the pits back into the barrel.

Shawn found a table covered with graffiti and sat down beneath a television that mutely flashed CNN's *World Report*. Kravetz could see the Kings of Israel Square on the television screen as he sat down. He could see blood on the pavement where the prime minister had been shot, and his stomach tensed.

"What are you doing here?" Kravetz said, still buzzing from nerves. Shawn had a history of surprising Stuart, and it usually meant trouble. They had been friends since second grade in Hebrew school when Shawn had dropped his pen so he could catch a peek up Miss Makhlabani's skirt and was smacked on the head with a ruler. Shawn had been his best friend, but that was a long time ago.

"Two Goldstars, *Motek*." Shawn snapped a finger in the air to get the waitress's attention. "Shit. She's the bomb."

Kravetz nodded his head, and thought women were always bombs, or chicks, or puss to Shawn.

"What am I doing here?" Shawn said, returning to Stuart's question. "I told you I'd come. I'm good for my word. You must be lonely, anyway. The literary exile. Shit, your parents haven't heard from you in months."

It was Kravetz's parents who had sent him to Israel in the first place, and it had nothing to do with Zionism, or making the desert bloom, or becoming a light unto nations. Five years earlier he and Shawn played in a punk band called Bitefinger Baby, and their drummer had stabbed someone at one of the clubs they were playing. His parents figured something bad was bound to happen if he stayed in the city, and he was too old for summer camp. So Kravetz and Shawn went to Israel.

They had spent a wild summer drinking together after their senior year of high school, as they traveled from the Golan Heights in the north to Masada and Eilat in the south. They had promised one day, stuffing notes into the Wailing Wall, that they would return to Jerusalem together.

"I kind of like the quiet," Kravetz said. "Gives me time to think."

"The last thing you want to do is think, my friend. Can I stay?"

"How long?"

"I love you, too, buddy. Do you remember when those skinheads tried to steal your Doc Martens?" Shawn said. "They called you a Jew and I convinced them that you weren't Jewish." Shawn poked Kravetz in the ribs and crushed him in a headlock. Kravetz gagged from the smell of his friend's Drakkar Noir cologne.

"But I am Jewish," he started to say before Shawn's bicep muffled his words.

"I saved you," Shawn said, letting go after a moment.

"Yeah. Thanks," Kravetz said, remembering that he once felt that Shawn and he were as close as brothers. "How long?"

"I don't know. Until I strike gold."

Shawn always seemed to get his way, and was not afraid to point out an obligation to him. He called in his favors again and again as if the debt lasted a lifetime.

"You know," Shawn said. "Until I milk this place for enough pics for a show."

A man and a woman sat together at a small table in the corner. The woman was crying. Kravetz wondered if the woman was crying because she and her boyfriend were breaking up, or whether she was mourning the death of the prime minister.

"I placed the ad," Shawn said after a moment. He lifted his silver briefcase onto the table and opened it. Kravetz could see another camera with a flash attached to it and a long zoom lens strapped in against the foam bedding. A small Polaroid camera lay beside the lens. Film canisters were strung across the top half of the case like a bandolier.

Kravetz remembered Shawn's idea for a spread for the upstart Heart-Shaped Jeans Company. He thought it was a stupid idea at the time: a bunch of beautiful, naked models frolicking in a heart-shaped pool, with their clothes crumpled and scattered around the deck like sex-deflated bodies. But now that he pulled a folded magazine out of his silver case and showed him the glossy ad, with the heading "Good Jean Pool," he had to laugh.

"If you will it, it is no dream," Shawn said, quoting Herzl with a smirk. He lit a filterless Noblesse cigarette. "It's brilliant, isn't it?"

"Yeah, it is," Kravetz said, and paused as the beers arrived. "Have you heard from Jana?" His voice almost caught in his throat.

"Nah, haven't seen her," Shawn said, sipping from his Goldstar. "This tastes like chlorine."

Kravetz was silent, and he thought of Jana again, his Janushka, and felt sick in his stomach and somewhat amazed that he could ever have been close enough to her to call her something as childish as Janushka. He wondered how she could be so far away and yet seem as if she were still in the room with him. Whenever he smelled patchouli oil, he always turned around to see if Jana had come looking for him.

Three Russians at the next table began singing an off-key, operatic rendition of "Hotel California." Jana hated Russians and never failed to give the finger to anyone on the road who drove a Lada.

"This place hasn't changed a bit," Shawn said.

"It's the only place open tonight," Kravetz said, thinking of the long lines of mourners making their way up to Mount Herzl that morning. "You're lucky."

"Always have been, always will." Shawn picked up his camera and looked through it. There was seldom a time that Kravetz remembered seeing Shawn without a camera around his neck or pressed to his face, so he wasn't surprised when Shawn pointed his camera toward a bald giant with a cinder-block head and thin purple lips who sat alone with his head down at a table across the room. "What's the deal with that guy?"

"That's Asher," Kravetz said. "He's a survivor. Sobibor."

"Fucking golem," he said and turned his camera toward a bearded man with a cell phone pressed to his ear. Shawn played with the lens as if he were focusing for a shot.

"That's Shmuelik. He used to be a rabbi, now he sells guns," Kravetz said, taking the first sip of his beer. "One of the guys who helped liquidate the Warsaw or the Lódź ghetto is living in Canada. Shmuelik knows a man who will pay any-one fifty thousand dollars to kill him."

"Shit, who wants to go to Canada?" Shawn said and spun in his seat, aiming his camera at Kravetz. "You look good. Better. Really."

"I don't know," Kravetz said. "Sometimes I'm thinking about what I want to eat or something, and suddenly Jana pops into my head. You know, the way she stood. I see trees that remind me of her. And sometimes I see a woman hold-ing a baby on the bus or something, and she doesn't even look like Jana, but you know —"

"Fuck her," Shawn said, finishing his beer. "You've got to be part animal, part machine." Shawn always felt empow-ered by paraphrasing punk-rock lyrics. He raised his camera to his face again, blinding Kravetz with his flash. "A fuckin' hot animal machine," he said, expelling a mouth full of smoke.

A Marriage Made in Heaven

A few days later, Kravetz sat on his sixth-floor balcony with a volume of Amichai's poems open in front of him. He read, "You are beautiful, like prophecies / And sad, like those which come true." And he thought of the time when he and Jana walked through the shallows of the water at Brighton Beach after visiting her aunt and eating some lardy meat prepared in the style of the "old country." Her hair was wet and she smelled seaweedy in the last purple light of day and she came up close to him almost shouting, "Hey!" as she pulled a damp pack of cigarettes out of her shorts pocket. "So 'cause I'm not Jewish or anything, does that mean you would never marry me?"

"You could convert," Kravetz had said, not sure if he was serious or joking.

The sun burst through the hard gray sky, its rays refracted like spotlights throughout the city. Kravetz looked out beyond the slope of Independence Park and the remains of the Mamilla Cemetery toward the Old City; the city that Twain had called the knobbiest town in the world with its crooked streets and countless domes, a city where Melville had written in disgust about the Crusader church being a sickening cheat where all is glitter and nothing is gold. But, looking toward the golden Dome of the Rock, Kravetz thought of how far he was from New York and Jana. He knew he would never run into her in the winding streets and alleys, and he felt glad for a moment.

That week Kravetz and Shawn sat up late drinking Goldstars and talking. Shawn knew Kravetz better than anybody, except Jana, and he built him up, saying, "You're a handsome guy. Look at those deep poetic eyes of yours. You're the handsomest guy."

Kravetz recounted every detail of his relationship to Shawn, told him how she kissed with her eyes open, how the blonde hair on her arms held the sun in the morning, and her secret nickname for him. He felt somehow lighter, as if he had unburdened himself of a great weight, and was thankful Shawn never once asked, "How was she?"

Kravetz was still a virgin, a junior in high school, when Shawn Silver had woken him with a drunken phone call at two in the morning to announce, "Gentlemen, that's lucky eighteen."

Lucky eighteen had always been sort of a joke between Shawn and Kravetz, but it seemed somehow appropriate that Shawn would invoke it after his eighteenth lay, since his first came shortly after his bar mitzvah. It was always the cheapskates who didn't have the class to buy them bar mitzvah gifts that handed them crumpled handfuls of money that always added up to eighteen dollars. Eighteen signified *chai,* or life, and was supposed to bring good luck.

Shawn wore his hair in a mohawk at the time, something Kravetz couldn't get away with, having curly hair that would have looked like a strip of carpet. Girls curious about Shawn always wanted to touch his hair.

He told Kravetz how he had gotten redheaded Jenn Liska drunk on peppermint schnapps, how she had ridden him like a horse in her parents' bed, with her tights rolled down to her knees, and how her breath tasted like an ashtray.

"Wow," Kravetz had said, half excited, half disgusted by the blow-by-blow details that made him hard.

"You'll get there, my son. You'll get there," Shawn said.

When Kravetz finally did sleep with a Montreal cocktail waitress ten years his senior that New Year's Eve, Shawn burst into the bedroom as soon as they were done, snapping the two strangers in bed with his Nikon.

"My boy Kravetz's first time," he had told the horrified waitress, laughing as she disappeared under the wrinkled sheets like a ghost.

Kravetz closed the book of poetry and felt the weight of loneliness all around him. Jana, he thought, "You are beautiful like . . ."

Kravetz had not heard the hum of the noisy elevator and the slam of its heavy door.

"Honey, I'm home," Shawn called, opening the apartment door. He appeared on the balcony a few minutes later, with the waitress from Elijah's Cup at his side. "Stuart, this is Ravit." She extended her hand, and Kravetz shook it, realizing she was the one wearing patchouli in the bar that night. She was tall and had dark hair, was maybe a Yemenite or Moroccan. She had a bright smile, and wore a loose red shirt.

"Ravit wants to be a star," Shawn said.

"Shut up, stupid," she said, hitting him lightly on the shoulder. Shawn pulled away and said, "Ow."

Kravetz knew now that they had had sex, or would soon have sex. He knew Shawn's gambit well — baiting, antagonizing, then feigning hurt to gain the girl's sympathies.

"Come on, we're going for a walk," Shawn said, adjusting his camera at his neck. "You can't study all day."

"You aren't religious, are you?" Ravit said. "I *hate* the religious."

"It's poetry," Kravetz said lamely.

"She hates the army, too. She just turned eighteen," Shawn said, grabbing a handful of her hair. "You're a nice girl," he said, leaning in close to kiss her.

"Fuck the army," she said, pulling away. "And fuck the crazy religious of this city. I'm going to Thailand next week." She laughed a loud, mannish laugh as she pretended to take a drag from a joint.

Kravetz noticed that her eyes seemed to be almost spinning with energy and were a deep, piercing green, the color of liquor-soaked lime rinds. He put his book down and said, "I gotta be at work in an hour."

Shawn popped open the back of his camera, reached into his vest, slid in a roll of film, and snapped it shut again without even looking at what he was doing, like a gunslinger loading up in the wild west. "Come on. Call in. Kids are united," Shawn said and stuck out his fist as he had so many times during their youth. Kravetz hesitated and then punched it with his own, adding his lines, "Never be divided."

A half an hour later they arrived at an ultraorthodox neighborhood that looked like an eighteenth-century Jewish ghetto. It was built like a stone fortress, with Yiddish posters plastered everywhere to the blackened walls. The streets were gray and potholed, and black-garbed men with beards and side curls walked through the crowded streets speaking in Yiddish. Shawn wore an open motorcycle jacket with a T-shirt that had "Social Distortion" written across the front. Kravetz noticed that Ravit walked with supreme confidence, taking dramatic, modelesque strides, not unlike Jana when she had felt the world was hers. Ravit spoke in a tuneless yet musical way and laughed, sometimes touching Kravetz on the shoulder.

"So serious," she said, frowning. "You must to have fun." She smiled.

They stopped before a sign that said, "**ATTENTION! YOU ARE NOW ENTERING THE ULTRAORTHODOX NEIGH-BORHOOD OF MEA SHEARIM. WOMEN ARE TO DRESS MODESTLY.**" The sign said that women should wear sleeves that reached at least to their elbow, and skirts that reached below their knees. Necklines were to be no lower than the collarbone.

Ravit undid the top two buttons of her cherry red shirt.

"Here we are," Shawn said as two men passed. "On your right you'll notice the latest ghetto fashions of the year of our Lord seventeen ninety-two. The bearded gentleman," and here Shawn laughed. Ravit hummed along to his commentary. "Oh, they're both bearded. The taller gentleman models a fur *streimel,* made out of the finest rat fur, trapped in the kitchens of Schmuel the baker."

Kravetz felt his stomach turn. "Shawn, what are you doing?"

Two more men passed and scowled at the three of them.

"You can't talk like that," Kravetz said.

"Why not? They don't speak English."

"They don't speak Hebrew, either," Ravit said. "Only to pray. God forbid you wipe your ass in God's Hebrew."

Now a woman pushing a baby carriage approached, her young daughter slowly walking at her side.

"Like a queen, her wig glistens in the sunlight, a wig this gorgeous you wouldn't dare cover with a bababababushka. . . ."

The girl lowered her head and sped up.

Shawn began to jump around singing, "Crucify-i-i-i-i me, Crucify-i-i-i-i me."

"Stop it," Kravetz said.

"Crucify-i-i-i-i me," Shawn continued.

Ravit grabbed him, pressed close, and whispered in his ear, "Be a good boy."

"You're gonna start a riot," Kravetz said, stepping away.

"Hey, that's cool," Shawn said.

"So I get stoned here instead of Thailand," Ravit said matter-of-factly.

"This isn't fucking Disneyland," Kravetz said.

"No. It's the fucking Holyland," Shawn said. "And you're playing Goofy."

At that moment, Kravetz hated Shawn, as he had hated him a thousand times before. But he knew that Shawn only wanted to have fun, and that he was trying to draw him out of his gloom. He really didn't understand, he hadn't seen the anger in the eyes of those men. And if Ravit was supposed to be a gift for him, like the Montreal cocktail waitress had been, he was not interested.

A gray-bearded man wearing a rumpled suit and black hat burst out of a building and charged toward them, calling Ravit a whore. His clenched fists looked like steel hammers, and he cursed at Shawn from beneath the sign. "She's not a whore," Shawn said. "She's the Virgin Mary." Kravetz was afraid somebody would get hurt, and pulled Ravit close to him by the shoulders. She was stronger than he thought, and pushed him away. Kravetz fell to the ground and he heard prayers from all around, as he scrambled to pick up his glasses. When Kravetz looked up again he saw that Shawn had his camera ready, aimed at the man, and that the man had covered his face with his hat to protect himself against breaching the Second Commandment forbidding graven images. And now Ravit unbuttoned the rest of her shirt, and pulled it open. She leaned close to the man, and blew a dramatic kiss at him, her bra and tattooed midriff bared for all to see.

Then the clickclickclickclickclickclick of Shawn's Nikon.

That was *A Marriage Made in Heaven,* and the beginning of FLICK Photos and Postcards.

Come Hither, Woman, Thy Breasts Are as Comely as Doves

Shawn thought it was so clever to spell the name FLICK in all capital letters, giving the illusion of the word FUCK as in the smudgy old comic books. He found a man named Sammi Shaloub who ran a camera store in East Jerusalem and who let Shawn use his darkroom for his black and white photos and would develop Shawn's color prints without asking any questions.

While Kravetz was busy studying, Shawn wandered through the city with his cameras trying to catch gold in his crosshairs. During his first week, he had been cursed in the Church of the Holy Sepulcher where he had an Australian girl, on the last leg of her three-year walkabout, slip out of her dress and lie on the Stone of Unction, smoking a cigarette where the body of Christ had been laid after he was removed from the cross. An Orthodox monk had chased him out with a burning censer into the stone courtyard, shouting "American" and "Fuck."

"It's like a dirty butcher's slab," Shawn had told Kravetz of the Stone of Unction, "and these pilgrims are tongue kissing it."

At the Dome of the Rock where the Prophet Muhammad had begun his night journey to heaven, where Muslims prostrate themselves in prayer, he snapped a Swedish girl he had just met, face to the ground, dress thrown over her head, bare behind in the air, praying to the mighty Allah. *The Ass of an Angel* even got a quiet "tsk, tsk" from Sammi Shaloub.

Shawn found two urchins throwing rotten fruit at frightened tourists outside of the Jaffa Gate and he convinced them to sell his provocative postcards for two dollars each, and before long he had a squad of six kids selling his photos throughout the city.

It was a rainy December day and Shawn had been staying with Kravetz for more than a month. The Old City was only twenty minutes from their King George Street apartment and they made the journey together about twice a week in search of sickeningly sweet Nablus-style *kanafi,* thick Turkish coffee, prickly pears, and any old trinket that caught their eyes. Shawn had bought a bullwhip on his last trip to the Old City and chased Kravetz all the way home, snapping the whip at him as he ran.

The streets were slick and luminous, seeming almost to glow in the gray light, and they passed a fruit stand and carpet and souvenir shops that sold olive-wood camels and manger scenes. They passed people in the streets, Arabs, Jews, and Christians, and Kravetz looked in every face as it passed, swearing that he saw something in each that reminded him of Jana. A boy carrying a large wooden tray of pita bread on his head bumped into Kravetz and mumbled something in Arabic that Shawn figured must be about Kravetz's mother. A shopkeeper shouted out "Special price," and waved a checkered kaffiyeh at Kravetz and Shawn as they descended deeper into the city. They reached a small mosque where, through the open door, they could see a man stretched out in prayer on the floor. Shawn had raised his camera and began to focus, but Kravetz said, "Let's go."

They arrived at a darkened shop where old black and white photographs dating from the time of the Ottomans and the British mandate hung in the window. Kravetz could see photos of a sheep market outside of Damascus Gate, slick water buffaloes trudging through the malarial Hula swamp, pilgrims dragging crosses down the Via Dolorosa, a man with an impossibly large mustache smoking from a water pipe. Shawn entered the store followed by Kravetz, and greeted the man behind the counter, who, it seemed, had been sleeping with his head in his arms.

"Welcome," the man said, jumping up.

The room smelled of old books and coffee, and a large color photo of the Dome of the Rock hung behind him. The man pulled back a curtain and disappeared for a moment, returning with a folded paper in his hand.

Shawn was looking at some color photographs of young boys throwing stones at Israeli soldiers. Kravetz could hear him chuckle, "Now that is what I call punk."

"Five hundred dollars," the man said, unfolding the piece of paper. "Only five hundred dollars. Look. Look," the man said.

Kravetz could see what looked like Hebrew letters and a bloodstain, with a hole in the middle of the page.

"You remember the prime minister," the man said. "Terrible thing."

"Robert Capa," Shawn said. "Bullshit pedestrian portraits. Look at this shit," Shawn said.

He flipped through a book of photos dating from the first days of the State of Israel. Pioneers, Kravetz thought, and smiled.

"Look," Shawn said. "Man building a fucking house, street scene Tel Aviv, ugly face no shirt, ugly face sun hat, rabbi, man with gun, eyepatch, ugly, ugly, ugly. These pictures are boring and ugly," Shawn said.

From the time he was a kid, Kravetz had always thought that Moshe Dayan in his eyepatch looked dashing. "And I suppose you are here to capture the beauty of Jerusalem's golden light," Kravetz said. "Its majestic architecture, from Herod to Süleyman the Magnificent . . ."

"No," Shawn said, shaking his head. "I'm here to be interesting. This shit is boring."

The man leaned in close to Kravetz, holding the page close to his face. He could see Hebrew lettering on the page.

"The Song of Peace," the man said.

"There will never be peace," Shawn said, picking up a book.

"Look," the man said. "The Song of Peace."

Kravetz remembered that the prime minister had been awkwardly singing the Song of Peace at the rally, only moments before he had been killed. He had folded the page and placed it in his breast pocket. "Only three hundred dollars," the man said.

"Let me see that," Kravetz said.

"No. No," the man said. "You can't touch it."

"Look at this," Shawn called. He waved an old leather-bound book. "A guide book."

"Two hundred fifty," the man said. "Look. The bullet hole. A Jewish bullet hole."

"Check this out," Shawn said, mumbling something in mangled Hebrew. "I have many gold pieces and many treasures . . ."

"That is a pilgrims' guide book to the holy city from the time of the Crusaders," the man said. He had a mustache that was just beginning to turn gray, and he wore a thick pair of glasses. He pulled Kravetz closer to him by the shoulder and said, "For you, two hundred fifty. That is his real blood. Smell it."

Kravetz turned away. He had lost sixty dollars in a shell game in Times Square when he was sixteen and had no interest in being ripped off again. He turned back to Shawn.

"What else does it say?"

Shawn laughed. "Here. This one is great. 'Come Hither, Woman, Thy Breasts Are as Comely as Doves.' Do you think that would work?"

"You've gotten away with worse," Kravetz said.

"You know, it's the Crusaders who fucked this place up in the first place," Shawn said. The man quietly folded the paper and put it back in his breast pocket. "You know, you've seen these Arabs with blond hair or blue eyes walking around. That's because they've been fucked by Crusaders, probably raped in the name of Christ."

"Come on," Kravetz said.

"You are living in the land of the perennially fucked," Shawn said. "A fantasy land of ghosts and fucking kooks."

"That's ridiculous," Kravetz said.

"The place was built directly on the ashes of the Holocaust."

"Bullshit," Kravetz said.

"It wasn't? So was that a picnic over there in Europe?

When the world stops feeling guilty about what happened over there, Israel will be wiped off the map."

"I don't believe that," Kravetz said.

"Let's go, man, this place stinks," Shawn said, walking toward the door.

"Yes, yes, you go," the man said. "But first you must buy. I have the bullets," the man added, reaching into his pocket. "Look how they have been flattened."

"So this is the golden Medina," Shawn said.

"Yeah, why not?"

"Bullshit. Even Herzl, your father of modern Zionism, said the only thing special about a Jewish state would be that the prostitutes would be Jewish, the thieves would be Jewish. . . ."

"It's not that . . ." Kravetz started to say.

"No, it's worse," Shawn said. "Living next door to terrorists, Scud missiles flying overhead, religious fanatics." He pulled the door open, looked at the man, and said, "This is a fucking garage sale. I'm outta here," Shawn said, curling his lips into a scowl.

Kravetz followed Shawn out into the street, not looking at the man as he left. Kravetz felt like arguing with Shawn, but by the time he caught up to him, Shawn was smiling. A pair of Arab women walked toward Shawn and Kravetz with their faces covered.

"Check it out, man." Shawn tried to say, "Come hither, woman, thy breasts are as comely as doves," as the two women passed.

"That's ancient Hebrew," Kravetz said. "They're not going to understand that."

The two women passed, ignoring Shawn and Kravetz. Shawn shouted down the street after them, "Your breasts are like two pillows, like two water balloons, two floppy, flapping, bouncing titties."

"Shut up," Kravetz said.

"They don't understand," Shawn said. "It's like the time we were in Montreal and we would point at our wrist, as if we're asking for the time."

"They knew you were asking them to suck your dick."

Now another woman walked toward them, carrying a string bag in her arms.

"Come on," Shawn said, "you try. We're going to get you laid."

"No way. That's obnoxious."

"Do you want me to get you laid or not?" Shawn said.

Two summers earlier, Jana had told Kravetz that she was going upstate for the summer solstice with some of her friends and that he couldn't come. "It's sort of a Baltic Bash," she had said.

"Tribalism," Shawn had said to Kravetz. "That cunt will never really accept you because you are not part of her tribe. Worse still, you're a Jew. She's probably cheating on you right now. Huh, some of that Polish kielbasa."

"You're an asshole," Kravetz said. "You're talking about my girlfriend?"

"Then why doesn't the bitch want you to go?"

Shawn was always putting doubts into Kravetz's head. At first Kravetz thought it was only jealousy, since Shawn never seemed to have a girlfriend for very long. But this time Kravetz was worried that something was going to happen. When Jana returned from the weekend away, she said the weekend was fine, but she drank too much. That worried Kravetz even more, and then he noticed the hair.

He told Shawn that she always had an inch-long black hair on her left breast, and when she came back from her trip it was gone.

"The bitch cut it off," Shawn said, "because she knew she was going to get fucked. I'll bet she shaved her bikini line, too, for the first time in a year."

That weekend Kravetz and Shawn got drunk at Haymakers and Shawn introduced Kravetz to Holly Jaundice, the singer of a local punk band.

"Have fun," Shawn called after them as they stumbled out of the bar.

And now in Jerusalem, Shawn called down the street after the woman, mangling the ancient Hebrew as he shouted.

"Shut up," Kravetz said. "Will you just shut up."

Christmas Day, Kravetz decided he should have called Jana to wish her a "Merry Christmas." Shawn had taken an Arab taxi to Bethlehem, hoping to catch some hysterical pilgrims in Manger Square. He still hadn't returned. Kravetz had picked up the phone several times and even dialed Jana's number, but always hung up before anyone answered. He thought that, somehow, thinking about her with the phone in his hand would be enough to make her pick up the phone and call him. He just wanted to hear her talk like old times, the way they used to. He wanted to apologize and to hear her say, "Me too." Sometimes his hand slipped down and he began to stroke himself, but he couldn't think of Jana. It just made him too sad, as if she were a ghost he couldn't get his arms around.

So You Should Never Forget

New Year's Eve, Kravetz and Shawn went to Elijah's Cup for drinks. The bar was packed, and loud Israeli music boomed from the speakers. They found a table near the back of the bar and sat down. Kravetz could tell that Shawn had slept with at least two or three of the girls they had passed by the way they stiffened as he walked past.

"To a new year," Shawn said. "This one's on me."

Kravetz noticed a graffito etched into the table — THE SEX LIFE OF THE EGYPTIAN SPHINX WAS LONELY / RESERVED FOR EGYPTIAN KINX — and said, "Don't worry about it."

"At least let me buy you a beer. You won't even let me give you money for rent."

"That's so I can throw you out whenever I want," Kravetz said, laughing.

Shawn did not laugh. "I'm buying you a beer."

They drank two or three beers, and Shawn hugged the waitress, saying, "Sylvester *Tov!*" Kravetz always felt good up until three beers, and looked around the room hopefully. It was only later that he began to feel gloomy.

A large crowd had gathered across the bar at the table where the infamous Asher was sitting in his usual seat. People stood on chairs and climbed onto each other's shoulders. They sang "Auld Lang Syne," and swayed rhythmically.

"What's going on?" Shawn said, grabbing his camera before Kravetz could answer.

Shawn pressed his head between a pair of thighs, and Kravetz could see that Asher had a skinny, blond German-looking guy pinned to the table. Now the crowd was chanting,

"Go! Go! Go! Go!" as Asher dipped a needle into a bottle of India ink. His eyes looked washed out and distant, as gray as dirty ice. Kravetz had heard stories about Asher, but never believed them. He raised his tattooed arm in the air, and jabbed the needle into the German's arm shouting, "Never forget! Never forget! Never forget!" The crowd roared with laughter, and Shawn burrowed his way through the crowd, onto the table. "I need light," he called. "Move back!"

But the crowd only moved closer, as Asher continued to jab away at the poor German's arm. Kravetz could hear Shawn saying, "Perfect. Fucking perfect," and imagined the title *So You Should Never Forget* appearing at the top of the postcard. And suddenly Asher was aware of his surroundings, and he reached up to grab Shawn by the neck with his cleaver-like hand.

"You," he said, pulling Shawn close. The German was still pinned to the table with his other massive hand. "Do you remember . . ."

"What?" Shawn said, his nasal voice rising.

"Do you remember?" Asher asked, pulling Shawn closer.

Kravetz tumbled onto the table over the top of Shawn, landing on Asher's arm. "Yes, he remembers! That's what the camera is for," Kravetz said.

"All right, break it up!" a black bouncer from Chicago said, pulling bodies away. "Everybody back to your tables before I bust some heads!" He turned to Asher. "Let's go," and he led Asher out of the bar.

"You saved me," Shawn said, running his fingers through his hair. "Fuck. I hope there was enough light."

"We're even, okay," Kravetz said.

Later, they were dancing at The Shelter, which was dec-
orated like a 1950s fallout shelter. It was a new year, and
Kravetz was drunk, as bodies spun all around him. He saw
Shawn jumping around to the Ramones' "I Wanna Be
Sedated" and felt his own blood pumping through him.
Shawn appeared a few moments later, sweating, with a girl on
his arm. "Stuart!" he shouted, "this is Amy!"

"Hi!" she said, extending her hand. She wore her
blonde hair in a long ponytail, red lipstick, and a short skirt.
The strobe light made her face look sunken and sickly.
"Wanna dance?" She pulled Kravetz into the swaying mass of
bodies, where soldiers' M-16s slapped against their arching
backs as they danced. Two girls wearing gas masks and bikinis
bounced past them.

Shawn called out, "You owe me, buddy!"

She put her arms around him and he smelled her beery
breath. He thought of Amichai's lines again: "People use each
other / as healing for their pain. They put each other / on their
existential wounds, / on the eye, on the cunt, on mouth and
open hand. / They hold each other hard and won't let go." And
he thought of taking her up his dark, noisy elevator, sliding his
hand in her pants as he fumbled for the keys to his apartment.
But it wasn't Jana, and she wouldn't say, "Thanks for fingering
me," and she wouldn't say, "I really love you," after he fucked
her. He turned to look in Amy's face but she was looking away
toward a group of her friends dancing on the bar.

A few minutes later, Kravetz pulled Shawn outside into
the cool damp air. His heart thumped so hard he thought he
might throw up. Shawn lit a cigarette and mopped his face
with the corner of his shirt. "What's going on?"

"I think I'm going to call Jana."

"What do you mean? Aren't you having fun?"

"Yeah, I guess," Kravetz said. "It's just, having my arms around that girl made me think of her. You know what I mean?"

"Bullshit," Shawn said as an army jeep drove past, its blue light flashing. He pulled his Polaroid out of his jacket pocket. He aimed the camera at Kravetz and snapped a shot.

"I'm going to call her," Kravetz said, ignoring the picture. He walked away from The Shelter.

"Do you want her to think you're weak?" Shawn called after him.

"I just want her to think of me."

"Come back here and look at this picture," Shawn called. "I don't want you to ever forget what the face of defeat looks like."

"I'm calling her," Kravetz said weakly, though he realized now that Shawn was right — he couldn't call her.

Dead Souls

It was a day before the Palestinian elections, and a cold January rain was falling from the gray sky. Jews both supporting and opposed to the Oslo peace plan took to the streets in full force. With Palestinians voting in their contested half of Jerusalem something was bound to happen, and Shawn planned to catch it on film. Shawn made Kravetz a breakfast of hard-boiled eggs, yogurt, and cucumbers. He wore no shirt when he served it to Kravetz. He had a Star of David that he had gotten five summers earlier at the port of Haifa tattooed on his right shoulder, a Misfits skull on his left. The tattoos looked strange to Kravetz now, though he had said they were cool when he first saw them, and had once wanted a local band's name tattooed on *his* arm.

"Do you have to smell everything before you eat it?" Shawn said.

Shawn smoked a cigarette as Kravetz ate.

"Do you mind if I come with you today?" Kravetz said, ignoring the question.

"Oh, now you want to be my assistant. You look like a groupie wearing that 'Peace Now' T-shirt."

"It's just I don't have classes today," Kravetz said.

The phone rang in the hallway, and Kravetz dropped his spoon into his yogurt. "You get it," he said to Shawn.

Shawn reappeared a few minutes later.

"Who was it?" Kravetz asked.

"Nobody."

"What do you mean, nobody? It had to be somebody."

"Shut up and eat," Shawn said.

"No, I want to know who it was. I pay the phone bill. Who was it?"

"Fine," Shawn said, lighting a cigarette and taking a slow drag. "It was Jana."

"What?" Kravetz shouted. "Why didn't you give me the phone?"

"She called for me," Shawn said.

"Bullshit," Kravetz croaked.

"It's true."

"She hates you," Kravetz said, his voice breaking. "She thinks you're arrogant and manipulative. She hates you." Kravetz covered his mouth with his hand, and then buried his head in the other hand. "You think you're fucking Sid Vicious."

"Ouch," Shawn said. "Are you coming, man?"

Kravetz didn't say anything.

"Fine. I'll see you later."

After Shawn left, Kravetz dialed Jana's number and it rang and rang, but nobody answered. It was the middle of the night in New York. He lay on his bed and stared at the ceiling, as the morning sun shined into his eyes, and he convinced himself that Jana must have called Shawn to speak about her and Stuart. They'd been together almost four years. You don't just love somebody and then never speak to them again.

Shawn stayed out all day taking pictures. Kravetz wandered into Shawn's dark room. He kept the iron shutters closed so the room smelled like an ashtray. Both carpets were rolled up in the corner, exposing the cracked, tiled floor. Half-finished incense sticks and *yahrtzeit* candles in small tin cups with the prime minister's face pasted on the front were strewn about the room. Shit, he even fucks to the light of memorial candles, Kravetz thought. He saw photos taped to the walls, and piled on his desk; a naked girl on a camel, another with some sheep, one with huge breasts and her arms outstretched as if she were waiting to be crucified. It's all crap, Kravetz thought.

Kravetz phoned Jana every night for three weeks, but nobody ever answered. When he heard her low voice on the machine he was reminded of conversations they had had. The first time she had said, "You have a beautiful prick," or the time she had innocently asked, "Do love and loathe mean the same thing?" He remembered the time she had cried to him about how she missed her grandfather in Riga, and how her voice had cracked, and how he had heard her accent seep in.

Some nights he heard girlish laughter from the next room and Shawn imitating their accents in his high nasal voice. One night Shawn knocked on Stuart's door and announced, as he swayed under the weight of alcohol, "You can now call me Doctor Professor Moses Kink. Here are my ten commandments of kink. . . ."

He had slathered gel in his hair so it stood up in devil-locks at the front like two horns.

"Shut the fucking door," Kravetz said. "What is it? A German or a Swede this time?"

"All by my lonesome tonight," Shawn said.

"Tell me," Kravetz said, sitting up in bed. "How many?"

"What?" Shawn said, smiling. "How many what?"

"Good night," Kravetz said, turning away from Shawn.

"All right, my son," Shawn said. He was never able to resist talking about himself. "The Doctor Professor Kink has had say, seventy-five, give or take. . . ."

"Give or take what?"

"Do you want to see the Polaroids?" Shawn said, twisting the horns on his head. He disappeared into his room for a moment. "I've got them all." He returned with a small shoe box cradled in his arms. He began flinging the photos at Kravetz. "Here. This one cried because she was too tight. This one bit. This one, this was the fat one." He kept firing the Polaroids at Kravetz. "This one was married, this one . . ."

"Shit," Kravetz said. He had only slept with one woman before Jana and one while he was with her.

Shawn's back stiffened and he became serious. "What? Since I was thirteen, that's less than ten a year. About point seven one two six five four women per month. Do the math. It's not that much. Seriously."

"That's crazy," Kravetz said.

"They meant nothing. They're dead. They're photos in a box."

"When are you going to leave?" Kravetz asked, surprising himself.

"What? 'Cause you're not getting fucked? That's weak. Take them all, then," Shawn said, throwing the entire box at Kravetz. He slammed his door and then opened it again. "When I've got enough for a show. That's when I'll leave."

Kravetz was shaking and couldn't sleep, so he went for a walk. He didn't even bother to pick up the Polaroids before he tiptoed out the door. He wore only a light T-shirt and shivered as he moved down the street in his checked slippers. A taxi passed and someone shouted out the window at him. He passed a lotto booth and for a moment wanted to smash the annoying face on the lotto ad. He knew that walking kept him from crying, so he walked as far as Rehavia Park and the Monastery of the Cross. Kravetz reached a clearing and lay on the damp ground beneath the stars. It seemed that the sky was lower than he'd ever seen it before, tilting dangerously close to the tops of trees and buildings, or maybe Jerusalem itself was rising into the heavens. Looking up into the blinking sky, he thought of Jana and how she had said that each star represents someone's soul and how she had once reached out toward the sky, grabbed at the darkness, and swallowed his soul in one gulp. And now he thought of Gogol and his trip to Jerusalem, and how after Gogol's return to Russia he had destroyed the second part of his masterpiece, *Dead Souls,* and then killed himself. Lying there in the grass, with the stars seemingly just out of reach, Kravetz never wanted to go home again.

King of the Pigs

It was a little after ten o'clock the next night when Kravetz entered Elijah's Cup. He and Shawn had made a silent peace, with the understanding that after Shawn had enough photos and a title shot that would burn into people's memories, he would return to New York. It was a Monday and Kravetz had studied all morning at the library on Mount Scopus then had gone straight to work at the cafe. He was damp with sweat and his shirt clung to his skin though it was only February. Shawn sat at a table in the corner with Shmuelik and a slim bearded man who wore a knitted *kippah* on his head. Elijah's Cup was silent, profoundly silent; Kravetz could hear the bearded man's New York accent and his laughter before the twanging thump and hand claps of Hebrew *mizrachi* music filled the room. The New Yorker was speaking loudly.

". . . you have them voting in East Jerusalem, next thing you know —"

The bearded man was cut off by Shmuelik. "Amalek as your next-door neighbor."

"Stuart, you know Shmuelik," Shawn said, offering Kravetz a seat at the table. "This is Mr. Berger."

Mr. Berger shook Kravetz's hand and popped an olive in his mouth. His beard was close cropped and he wore an expensive gold watch on his wrist. "I've still got to drive to Efrat tonight. I'd better be going." He stood up and Kravetz could see a pistol in his belt.

"Nice to meet you," Kravetz said.

Shmuelik, too, stood up and walked Mr. Berger to the door.

"So, what do you think?" Shawn said, sipping his beer.

"What do I think of what?" Kravetz said.

"Do you know where I can get a pig?" Shawn asked.

"What are you talking about?" Kravetz could see Shmuelik and the bearded man embracing as they parted ways.

"A pig," Shawn said. "You can't get a fucking pig in Israel. Isn't it illegal or something to breed them?"

"It's illegal to breed them *on* the land," Kravetz said. "But I know some kibbutzim in the north who have them on platforms, you know, *above* the land."

"Fuckin' A. Russians I bet."

"What do you need a pig for?"

"Business," Shawn said, hoisting his drink.

"Hey, Shawn? I was thinking . . ."

"Don't talk about her. Tonight we're celebrating."

The next morning Shawn was gone by the time Kravetz woke up. He didn't return for a few days, and when he finally burst through the apartment door whooping, "My masterpiece!" Kravetz was not surprised. He knew Shawn was up to something.

"That was the easiest ten grand I ever made. Come on, you want to help me put them up?"

Kravetz didn't raise his eyes from his book.

"Put that book down," Shawn said. "Look!"

He held a glossy full-color poster in his hand with a pig wearing an Arab headdress, propped up on his hind legs. There was Arabic writing across the top of the poster, and the words "MUHAMMAD, KING OF THE PIGS" written in English along the bottom.

"Holy shit!" Kravetz said. "What the hell is that?"

"Ten thousand dollars," Shawn said, smiling. "Two days work. And bacon, too."

From the look in the pig's eyes, Kravetz wondered if Shawn had drugged it.

"Mr. Berger?" Kravetz asked.

"Yeah," Shawn said. "The Security Council of Judea and Samaria. They've got deep pockets. If you help me poster, there will be something for you, too."

"Poster?"

"Yeah, man. I've got five hundred to put up around the city by tomorrow morning."

"Give me that," Kravetz said, lunging at the poster.

"Why, you want to help?" Shawn said, extending the poster. Kravetz reached for it. "Psyche!" Shawn said, and ran down the hall. "Are you going to help or aren't you?"

Suddenly, Kravetz felt old, like he was Shawn's father. Maybe he was making too big a deal about things. He had become so serious since Jana had left him, and spent too much time with his nose buried in books. He carried Amichai's poetry with him everywhere he went, as if it were a bible of heartbreak. "Good luck," Kravetz said, flopping back onto his bed.

"Shukran, habib," Shawn called in Arabic. "Thanks, pal."

Neither Shawn nor Kravetz heard the bomb when it went off three days later; bus number eighteen, a route that went through the heart of the city, blown up during the morning rush hour by a suicide bomber. The lucky number eighteen, or *chai* for life. Twenty-four people dead. Kravetz thought it was ironic that of all the numbers, of all the bus routes to choose, the bomber chose the one symbolizing life.

When Kravetz woke Shawn and told him the news, Shawn could only fumble for his camera and say, "Shit. Missed it."

Kravetz remembered a line from Amichai's poetry about the three languages of the holy city: Hebrew, Arabic, Death.

The Bombshell

In the days following the bombing, Shawn followed Kravetz to the rally at Zion Square, not to pay condolences to the dead and maimed, but to catch someone with their pants down.

When a man led a sheep on a leash into the square, chanting, "Like sheep to the slaughter. We're not sheep!" Shawn ran to him, but was stopped by a border policeman who said, "No photos. Only press."

Though people were told not to gather in large groups, the crowds chanted and called for peace. Heavily armed soldiers snaked through the crowds; two soldiers stood at each bus stop, checking bags for bombs.

"It's just like Europe before the war," Shawn said. "Can't you see the writing on the wall. This is *Kristallnacht* all over again."

"So leave, if you're so afraid," Kravetz said. "Go home."

"Why don't you?" Shawn said, blowing smoke in Kravetz's face. "Huh?"

"This is home," Kravetz said.

"Fuckin' idealist."

"Yeah, so?" Kravetz said, clenching his fists. He felt like he was in fourth grade all over again. "Go home, if you're afraid."

"I never said I was afraid, asshole. It's just, violence breeds hysteria," Shawn said. "And hysteria makes good photos. I'm going for a drink."

Kravetz went home and lay on his bed, throwing a tennis ball against the ceiling. He could hear a man coughing from the floor below, deep retching coughs that went on for minutes before he was silent. Kravetz wondered if the man had died. He picked up the shoe box from under his bed and began flipping through Shawn's Polaroids. The photos looked so cheap, bad lighting and red eyes, most of the women mugged for the camera and looked drunk out of their skulls. He thinks he's fucking Gene Simmons, Kravetz thought. The group seemed to be made of equal parts blonde and brunette with a redhead or two thrown in. Kravetz recognized some of the girls but could not recall their names. One of the pictures was stuck to the back of another and he pulled it off.

It was Jana.

Kravetz went numb. He hadn't seen her since May and her face, puckered and drunk, looked cheap and foreign. Could it really be her? She hated Shawn, thought he was a phony and an asshole. And suddenly, without any warning, he just burst out, one loud wrenching cry, his eyes burned, his throat swollen, his saliva as thick as cotton.

He didn't even hear Shawn come in. He was breathing heavily, as if he had taken the stairs.

Shawn walked forward and took a deep breath that made him look like a bulldog. "You're not going to cry again over the Slovakian slut. She's a Jew killer," Shawn said.

Kravetz could tell that Shawn was drunk. "You found her," Shawn said.

Through blurry eyes Kravetz could not tell if Shawn was smirking or biting his lips from nerves.

"Why?" Kravetz said.

"These Slavic bitches," Shawn said. "All of them, Russians, Latvians, Czechs, every last fucking one of them — Jew killers."

"What are you talking about?" Kravetz said.

"You know what I'm talking about. You know how they killed our grandparents and our great-grandparents, and their parents. Made us live in ghettos." Shawn slurred most of these words out. "Any Jew who consorts with these types must hate himself, must have a death wish."

"But I loved her, and she loved me," Kravetz said.

"Bullshit. Take a look at yourself, Poochie. What kind of Jew would fuck a pogromist pig?"

"She was going to live with me. I don't know."

"You scared the shit out of her. You're too fucking serious and intense," Shawn said. "You pressured her. Practically forced her under the weight of guilt."

Kravetz didn't say a word. He had never been so wounded in his life before.

And now Shawn's voice became as hard as it had ever been. "I did it for you, man. I don't give a shit about her. Yeah, she called a few times trying to find you, but I never told her shit. I told her to fuck off, but she kept calling. Don't you understand we're on the same side here. I only did it to get back at her for you."

"Get out!" Kravetz shouted. "Get out of here! I want you out of here now!"

"Don't you get it?"

Kravetz threw the tennis ball at Shawn, then threw the half-empty box of Polaroids at him.

"Don't freak out. I did it for you, man. The cunt hurt

you, so I got her back. Come on." Shawn stuck out his fist and said, "Kids are united . . ."

"Get the fuck out of here," Kravetz said, batting his hand away. "Asshole! Fucking grow up."

"Bro, listen . . ." Shawn began to say.

"Go to sleep," Kravetz said. "I don't want to see your face in the morning."

Lucky 18

The next morning Kravetz was woken by a ground-shaking boom that rattled even the walls of his apartment. He lay in bed, unable to move, with the horrible silence filling his ears, thinking, "There're no sirens, so it can't be," and when he heard the sirens he thought, "That's not enough sirens for a bombing." And he prayed, or muttered what he thought was a prayer. He could hear Shawn in the next room, shouting, "Get dressed, let's go!" as the sirens wailed outside. Shawn burst into Stuart's room, buttoning his pants. His shirt was open and his camera hung around his neck. He threw open Stuart's steel shutters, and they could hear sirens racing down Azza Street, and others from the Hadassah Hospital on Mount Scopus moving toward the rising smoke on Jaffa Street, just at the other side of Independence Park.

"Get up, bitch," Shawn said. "We're going to miss the whole thing."

"It's bus eighteen again," Kravetz said. He felt hollowed out inside, and could barely breathe. He thought of Jana, and Shawn thrusting against her, and Jana with her eyes wide open, saying, "Uh-huh. Uh-huh, uh-huh, uh-huh, uh-huh," as he pushed into her. Kravetz imagined Shawn's tongue all over Jana like some absurd pink fish flopping about her body. Then he thought of the bombing, and imagined bodies scattered about the streets like torn-up rag dolls. He didn't want to move. He just wanted to close his eyes and open them again to the misty rain falling out of the gray sky.

Shawn pulled Kravetz out of bed onto the floor. "Let's go," he said, his voice rising nasally. Kravetz wanted to run at Shawn, throw him to the floor, and strangle him, squeeze every breath of life out of him. But then he thought of the twisted metal of bus eighteen, and cried out, "It's your fault! It's your fault, you fucker!"

Shawn was rushing around the room, grabbing Stuart's clothes. "We've still got a five-minute walk, let's go!"

"They were throwing stones in East Jerusalem, calling for a holy war," Kravetz shouted as he pulled on a pair of pants. "A fucking jihad because of your picture."

"Have you ever seen a dead person before?" Shawn asked calmly, lighting a cigarette.

"Well," Kravetz said. He had thought that Jana was as good as dead to him, but he knew she still walked and talked and kissed and fucked. Out the window he could see smoke rising into the sky to meet the gray clouds. And he wondered what lay beyond the clouds.

"Boo!" Shawn said, waving his arms in Stuart's face. "Let's go."

A moment later Kravetz was dressed and he was smoking one of Shawn's cigarettes. He felt delirious, almost drunk with some sort of sickened excitement. No, he never had seen a dead person before and he wondered at what moment the soul left the body, and whether if you watched carefully enough you could see it escaping its earthly bonds.

They ran through the park and the sirens kept coming from all around. Shawn tripped over a stone at the entrance to an old Muslim tomb where men traded blow jobs after dark. He lay in the grass. "I'm dying, Stuey! I'm dying!"

"Come on," Kravetz said.

"Go on without me."

"Your lens cap is off, dick," Kravetz said, running ahead.

"Wait for me, you freak."

The rain was falling harder when they arrived at Jaffa Street. Hundreds of people crowded around the steaming carcass of the bus, which was flattened and twisted like some giant insect. A police line pushed the crowds back. Religious men dressed in black shook their fists, chanting that peace with the Arabs is suicide. Men dressed in white jumpsuits were picking through the debris for body parts. Kravetz had read about these men in the newspaper the past week, how it was their job to gather every hair, tooth, and drop of blood for a proper Jewish burial. Atop the Generali Building *Hesed shel Emet* volunteers scraped body parts from the face of a winged stone lion. Shawn stood on a garbage can and pulled Kravetz up with him. Kravetz held Shawn around the waist and could feel his warm behind against him. All the windows were shattered along Jaffa Street. A woman hung her head out the window and wailed.

"There's one," Shawn said. "Look."

Kravetz could see a black charred body lying on the road behind the bus and then another, a woman tangled inside the bus, beneath a seat back. He could see her colorful wool dress hiked up high on her bleeding thigh, and he swore he saw her move, just for a second. He saw a green apple on the ground nearby that seemed to be miraculously untouched.

"I'm going down there," Shawn said, jumping from the garbage can.

"What? How?" Kravetz said.

Shawn smiled and flashed him his fake foreign press ID card and said, "Don't leave home without it." And he ran off through the crowd.

Kravetz was too stunned to move and just stood where he was until a man climbed up on the can next to him and whispered in his ear, "Oslo is dead."

Stuart's throat clenched, as if he would cry, but he could only cough. Shawn had weaseled his way through the barrier and had moved in close to the bus, snapping shots next to CNN, UPI, the AP. This was it, Lucky Eighteen, the shot they'd both been waiting for. And Shawn was down in front at the second bus eighteen bombing, kneeling next to the lady with the wool dress. Kravetz could see him pull away the seat back and before Shawn turned to flash the thumbs-up sign, Kravetz could see there was no upper part of her body. He leaned over and threw up, a thin viscous fluid that tasted like tobacco, like Jana's kisses, like five thousand years, like the dying peace process. When he looked up again, Shawn had it in the can, his centerpiece shot, the woman with her skirt hiked up, his prize winner, a lament, or celebration of . . . something they didn't fully understand.